A
Place
for Allie

A Place for Allie

MARY CAREY

DODD, MEAD & COMPANY • New York

1 2 3 4 5 6 7 8 9 10

Library of Congress Cataloging-in-Publication Data

Carey, Mary.
A place for Allie.

Summary: When their happy home life in Nova Scotia
is tragically interrupted and their lives are forever
changed, twelve-year-old Allie and her little sister
take drastic steps to try to gain control over their
future.

[1. Sisters—Fiction. 2. Nova Scotia—Fiction]
I. Title.
PZ7.C2143Pl 1986 [Fic] 85-16005
ISBN 0-396-08583-0

JUVENILE

To Mary Alice

A
Place
for Allie

One

The window was open and spring was coming in. It was the chill, damp spring that always came late to Nova Scotia, but there was promise to it. Allie could smell newly turned earth, and she knew that if she stood up and looked out she would see the apple trees beside the lane swelling with buds.

But there was Mother, and she was saying, "You're doing it all wrong. It will be lumpy. Now pay attention!"

Allie was twelve and she was learning to mend socks.

"Can't I do it later?" she asked. "Today's the first nice day we've had."

"You have to grow up sometime," replied Mother. "Today's as good a time to start as any."

She took the sock from Allie. It was Papa's sock and there was a big hole in the heel. Allie watched Mother smooth the sock over the darning egg and send the needle weaving back and forth across the hole. "There!" she said, pulling the thread gently so that it would lie flat and not pucker. She handed the sock back to Allie. "Where is your sister?"

"Gertrude's fishing, and I wish I was," replied Allie. But the basket was filled with socks, and each sock had a hole. It would be dark before she finished—if she ever did finish. Allie tried to weave the thread across the hole as smoothly as her mother had done it. She felt herself clumsy, and she grew tense waiting to hear Mother say so. But then there was the sound of a carriage in the lane, and Mother turned her head, listening. Allie stood up and looked out.

It was Aunt Nonie with her tired, sway-backed old mare and her warped, squeaking buggy. Allie was not fond of Aunt Nonie, but today she was glad to see her. Even Nonie was better than worn socks.

Mother evidently did not think so. She sighed and put the darning basket aside and got up to close the window. Allie knew why. Aunt Nonie was fearful of drafts, which Mother believed were only bits of fresh air. When Aunt Nonie was exposed to a draft, she might manage to catch cold, and if she did she would speak of it for months afterward.

"Put the kettle on, Allie, and don't fill it so full that it takes all afternoon to boil."

Allie went out of the chill parlor and across the hall to the big warm kitchen where the black stove made comfortable noises. She encouraged the stove with more wood from the bin, and she filled the kettle with water from one of the buckets that stood on a bench near the stove.

The front door opened and Allie heard her mother say something to Aunt Nonie. Then Aunt Nonie was at the kitchen door, looking in at Allie with eyes as hard and bright as new marbles. She did not greet Allie, for she seldom spoke directly to children. She spoke above them or to one side of them, as if they were deaf.

"She's growing tall," said Nonie now. She looked past Allie's ear.

"It happens," replied Allie's mother. "Nonie, why don't we go into the parlor? Allie can bring the tea when it's ready."

Nonie ignored this. She came into the kitchen, holding her skirts clear of the floor, and sat down at the kitchen table. "I saw John in Guysborough today," she announced.

"He's often there," said Allie's mother.

Allie took cups and saucers from the cupboard. She did not look at her mother. She did not have to. She knew that Mother was frowning, wondering why Nonie had come. Was she there to learn something? Or had she come to deliver some troublesome bit of news?

Allie went on with her preparations for tea, wondering how Uncle Matt could ever have married anybody like Nonie. Mother said that Nonie had a fresh, sweet look to her when she was young. She had lost it soon enough, however, with her grasping ways and her prying into other people's affairs. "If she had a chick or a child to look after, she wouldn't have so much time to watch what others do," Mother was fond of saying.

"I didn't know you were planning to hire a boy." Aunt Nonie watched Mother, her eyes sharp.

"A boy?" echoed Allie's mother. "Why, no. Whatever made you think we might? Tom Anderson does what needs doing here."

"If you aren't hiring a boy, why was John buying trousers? Boy's trousers, and rubber boots."

Allie caught her breath. Nonie must have seen Papa in Uncle Matt's dry goods store, and of course she had noticed the trousers and the boots. And of course she immediately had to run to find out about them.

Allie felt her mother's eyes on her. She turned away and went quickly into the pantry to get some jam.

"Probably Tom Anderson needs trousers." Allie's mother sounded as if her husband bought trousers for the neighbor boy every day. "Tell me, Nonie, how has your stomach been these past weeks?"

It was a wonderful question. It was perhaps the only question that could have made Aunt Nonie leave off inquiring about the trousers. Nonie loved to talk about her stomach, which was delicate. "It's so difficult," she said, with one hand at her waist to show just where it was difficult. "One has to be so careful of every little thing that comes to the table. And lately I've been having these shooting pains behind my eyes. Do you suppose there could be any connection?"

Mother did not even attempt to answer this, for the tea had brewed and the toast was buttered. She poured a cup and passed it to Nonie and said, "It's wonderful the way you bear up. But can't Doctor MacDonald give you anything?"

"Some little powders, but they don't really help. Matt

says there's a new doctor in Halifax who's done some clever things. He thinks I should see him."

Allie carefully did not smile. Of course Uncle Matt would love to have Aunt Nonie off in Halifax for a while. With Nonie away he might get out of the dry goods store for a few hours. He and Papa might even go fishing together.

When the toast was eaten, Allie brought out the loaf cake her mother had baked that morning. It had currants in it, and when Mother began to slice it Aunt Nonie's eyes lighted. "How grand!" she said. "I'll have just a crumb." She went on to eat two pieces, and by that time the trees were throwing long shadows across the lane. Nonie stood up and pulled her shawl around her.

"So glad you came," said Allie's mother.

"It's always good to see you, Nell." Aunt Nonie barely smiled. She turned to go out, and again she held her skirt clear of the floor.

"It's clean!" Allie said suddenly.

"What's clean?" asked Aunt Nonie.

"The floor. Tom scrubbed it yesterday, so you don't need to hold up your skirt."

"Allie!" cried her mother.

Aunt Nonie sniffed and hitched her skirt still higher.

Allie's mother stood in the doorway to watch Nonie turn her carriage toward Guysborough. "Allie, whatever possessed you?" she scolded. "You know better than to say things like that to Nonie."

"Well, she acts as if we're dirty or she doesn't like us."

"She probably doesn't like us. I haven't noticed that she's fond of *any* of Matt's family. Do you care?"

"I guess not. But Uncle Matt always looks so beaten down and . . . and maybe he'd be different if she were different. Maybe he'd be . . . happier."

"Poor Matt!" Allie's mother sighed, then stepped back and closed the door. She looked sharply at Allie. "Boy's trousers and rubber boots?"

Allie felt her face get red.

"You knew about that, Allie. You're plotting behind my back!"

"Mother, no! Really, we're not, but . . ."

"You are not going to rig yourself up in trousers and go off to the island with your father! It's too dangerous!"

"Mother, I'll be careful!"

"Of course you will, for you won't go. I won't hear of it, and now we'll have no more talk about it."

"But Mother . . ."

"Not another word!"

Mother whirled and went into the kitchen and began to pile things in the dishpan. Allie stood in the hallway and wondered whether to go in after her or to go upstairs out of the way. Just then Gertrude came in.

Gertrude was nine and perpetually grubby. Her shoes were wet now, and so was the hem of her skirt, but she had two trout. Allie trailed after her to the kitchen.

"Ugh!" cried her mother. "Look at you! And you don't even *like* fish!"

"Papa likes fish," said Gertrude. She tugged at her hair, which had burrs in it.

"That's fine," said Mother. "Who's going to clean them?"

"I will," offered Allie, glad of the chance to get away. She took the fish and went out to the back step. Her father had taught her to clean fish and to be careful not to slice a finger as she did it. She slit the trout along the underside, scooped out the entrails, and carried them to the trash pit. Then she drew a bucket of water from the well and washed the fish and washed her hands. She did not go back into the house. Instead she sat on the steps outside the kitchen door and watched the lane. She tried not to notice the air growing chill as the sun went down.

It was almost dark when John Hughes came home at last. He drove briskly. His buggy did not creak, and his horse did not plod along like Aunt Nonie's poor tired mare. Maude pranced instead.

Allie went to the gate as her father reined the mare in. He bent toward her, and she saw him smile under his big, dark mustache. "Well, Allie! And what are you doing out here in the cold?"

"Papa, Mother knows. Aunt Nonie was here today. She saw you buying the boots and the trousers."

"Oh, blast!" said Papa. "I was afraid she'd noticed. Well, don't worry. We have three whole days. It will be all right."

"I don't think so," said Allie. "Not this time."

"Leave it to me. Now you go into the house before you catch cold, and I'll put Maude in for the night."

Allie went, taking the trout with her. Her mother was

15

at the table slicing potatoes. "You've been out there scheming with your father," she said.

Allie did not deny it. There was no use denying it. In silence she put the trout on the bench next to the water buckets. Then she started upstairs to the room she shared with Gertrude.

"Don't be up there all night," said Mother. "It's almost time to set the table."

Gertrude was sitting on the bed in her petticoat with her bare feet tucked under her. "Did Papa get the things?" she wanted to know.

"Yes, but Aunt Nonie saw him and she told Mother. Mother says I can't go."

"Don't worry. Papa will fix it. You'll go, and when I'm a little bigger I'll go."

"Don't be so sure." Allie was surprised to feel a lump in her throat. She knew she should not cry just because of a disappointment, but she wanted to cry anyway.

A door opened and closed downstairs. Her father's voice boomed. Papa often talked loudly when he had done something Mother might not approve.

Allie stole to the top of the stairs, and Gertrude got off the bed and came after her. "It's sneaky to listen," she whispered.

"I know," Allie whispered back.

The girls heard their mother give a little shriek of delight. "John, you're mad!"

"Don't you like it?" Papa demanded.

"Certainly I like it. It's beautiful! But it must have cost . . ."

16

"Cost? You sound like Nonie! Give her a peacock and she'd put it in a coop and wait for it to lay eggs."

"I'm *not* like Nonie!"

"I know. You're prettier!"

Papa's voice was soft. Then there was silence, and then Mother laughed. Papa was kissing her. Allie felt a little forlorn. When Papa and Mother were like this, it was as if she and Gertrude were not important.

Allie looked at Gertrude. Gertrude did not look at all forlorn. She was grinning, and she nodded in a satisfied way. "See? I told you. Papa's smart. He'll fix it. Wait and see."

Two

"Even if it turns out that you can't go," said Gertrude, "maybe you shouldn't care too much. It isn't really a desert island. You won't be a castaway, and you won't pick coconuts and catch fish for your dinner."

Allie smiled. Gertrude had read *Robinson Crusoe* that winter, and then had been disappointed when Papa confessed that his island had no coconut trees, but only ordinary oaks like the ones in the woods beyond the pasture.

Allie and Gertrude were walking home from school the day after Aunt Nonie's visit. They were hopping over the puddles in the road, or going around the bigger ones, and Allie could feel the sun warm on her face. They were six miles from the sea, but the wind that blew cold on her back had the feel of the ocean.

There had been no more talk of the island last night.

Mother had sat at dinner with a proud smile on her face and a new pin at her throat. It was a circle of gold, and there were red stones set in it. Mother was pleased with it, as she was pleased with all of Papa's gifts, from the amber beads to the beautiful porcelain stove in the dining room—the stove that had been ordered all the way from Holland.

In spite of the gift, however, Mother had given no sign that she had changed her mind about the trip to the island. Several times during the meal Allie had felt her mother's gaze upon her, and it had made her uneasy. It had made Gertrude doubtful. Perhaps this time Papa would not prevail.

"We don't even own the island," said Gertrude now. "Not really."

"We lease it from the government," said Allie. "Leasing is almost the same as owning. So long as you pay, it's yours."

Papa had signed the lease three years before, and for three years he had talked of the island, and had said that Allie and Gertrude could go with him to see it when they were old enough—when they could be trusted to be careful in the boat. In the springtime early, before the fishermen came, he would take them. Allie would go first, and then Gertrude. They would see the perfect island. It was small enough so that Papa could walk around it in an hour, and far enough from land so that a man could believe himself in charge of the world when he was there.

There had been nothing built on the island when Papa first signed the lease—nothing but a little dock put up by some long-departed tenant. Papa had hired men to work with him, and he had built drying sheds and shacks along the beach. The fishermen who put out from Canso in dories could bring their loads of cod to the sheds to be dried and salted, and they could spend their nights in the snug little shacks. There would be no need for the fishermen to make the long pull back to the harbor each night. In return for the use of the island, Papa got part of their catch. He did not take it in cod, either. He took it in money, for there was no use being in charge of the world with empty pockets.

Papa liked money.

He did not like it the way old Mr. Connell liked it. Mr. Connell liked money too much to spend any. He was said to have heaps of gold and silver coins hidden under his kitchen floor, but he also had holes in his boots and patches on his coat. Papa liked money because it was a way to know a thing was well done. He said that when you made money doing something, you knew you had done it well.

And making money was just part of the game. Papa liked to spend it too. "A man who can't spend can't make," he said, whenever Mother worried about the way the dollars disappeared.

Mother would be quiet then, for she knew she lived finer than most of the women around her. Before he ever met Mother, Papa had borrowed money to build the sawmill that now stood at the end of the lane. For a while he had run the mill himself, turning rough logs to finished lumber, buying timber from farmers and selling smooth white planks. And when the mill had paid for itself twice over, Papa had grown bored with it and had hired a man to run it. Then he had leased the island. It was the rents from the island that had paid for the brood mare. Now the mare had been bred, and Allie knew that Papa looked forward to the birth of the first foal. She also knew that he would never be satisfied with one mare. Papa talked of what one must do to raise the finest carriage horses.

"Can't you farm the land like other men?" Mother sometimes asked.

"I'd rather put to sea in a lead canoe," Papa always answered.

So the farming, such as it was, was looked after by Mother. No matter that she had lived all her life in the town of Antigonish. She had come to the farm as a bride and had set herself to learn about land and livestock. Now she knew when the hay was ready for cutting, the apples for picking, and the potatoes for digging. She churned the butter and made the cheese. She could card the wool from their own sheep when James Anderson sheared for her.

Not that Mother ever put her own hand to a clod of earth. James Anderson did that, coming across the fields from the next farm when he was summoned. But it was Mother who summoned him, and Mother who was careful always, for she had grown up in a narrow little house where there were too many young ones and never enough money. Her own father had not been like Papa. He had not been a good hand to make, and when he died it was Mother who had had the worry of staying on in that narrow house while her brothers and sisters went off. It was Mother who had had to see to taking care of her own mother. And then one of her sisters had come home a widow, and had brought three children with her, so again there were too many young ones in the narrow little house. To hear Mother tell of it, she had married to get away from children.

That was not true, of course. She had married because there was no way to refuse Papa, once he came asking, and she was proud of him, even if his extravagance did frighten her sometimes.

Allie and Gertrude turned from the road onto the lane that crossed the Hughes property. There was a wagon rumbling down from the sawmill with a pile of fresh cut boards. Mr. Sloane was holding the reins, and when he saw Allie and Gertrude he put his hand to the brim of his hat in a quick salute. They smelled the clean smell of the new lumber as the wagon passed.

The big doors of the sawmill were open wide, and Mr. Kelly stood there watching Mr. Sloane drive off with the lumber he had bought. When Allie and Gertrude came up the lane with their books, he waved and grinned.

Allie waved back, feeling her spirits lift as they often did at this place. She could look beyond the square, weathered bulk of the sawmill and see the fields. Today they were green after long months of snow and wet. The blossoms were like faint pink frosting on the apple trees, and up the lane, halfway between the road and the wooded upper slopes that circled the valley, there was the house where Allie had been born. She could just see the roof beyond the trees. She could not see the barn that was across the lane from the house, but she could picture it in her mind. And beyond the barn, at the very end of the lane, was the big house where Papa himself had been born. Grandpa had built that house, and he had lived there most of his years. Now Grandpa was dead and Grandma lived there by herself.

Halfway up the lane Gertrude and Allie rounded a bend in the road and saw Grandma coming toward them. Shep the dog stalked by her side.

Grandma stopped when she saw the girls, and the dog stopped too. "Gertrude!" Grandma called. "Mary Alice! Come here!"

Allie ran up past her own gate. She wanted to hug Grandma, but she did not. The old lady was frail and easily made unsteady on her feet. She held out her hand and Allie took it, feeling it so thin there seemed no flesh to it at all. Indeed, there was not much to Grandma that a stout wind might not blow away, and when Allie stood beside her she felt herself tall. She wondered if Grandma might not be held upright by her corsets.

"Are you coming to see us?" Allie asked.

"Who else would I be coming to see? I maun speak to your father, for the lane is rough after the thaw."

"I think Papa's in Guysborough," said Gertrude.

"Then I'll speak to your mother." Grandma frowned at Gertrude. "Ye do get yerself into a tangle," she said.

Gertrude pushed back her hair. "Papa says I'm like you."

"And what would he mean by that?" asked Grandma.

"He means you were wild. He says Grandpa told him."

"Tis a sad thing when yer sins come back to plague ye in old age," said Grandma, but she was smiling.

Allie smiled too, knowing the story. Grandma had come to Nova Scotia from Scotland long years ago. She was to marry a man named McPherson. He was a Catholic who had come from Inverness to find his fortune in the new world. He had opened a shop in Halifax and had thrived, so he had sent for his sweetheart, and that sweetheart was Grandma. But the first person Grandma had seen when she set foot on the wharf had been Grandpa. Not that he was Grandpa then. He was Hugh Hughes, and a Protestant, but Grandma had married him just three weeks later—in spite of the Protestant part of it—and too bad for poor McPherson.

Allie opened the gate for Grandma. Mother had seen them coming and was waiting in the doorway.

"Well, Ellen?" said Grandma. She went up the steps and held out her cheek for her daughter-in-law to kiss.

Shep flopped down in the dooryard. He was a long-haired creature who had a collie somewhere in his background—and doubtless a few other breeds as well. He had lived with Grandma for as long as anyone could remember, and he knew full well that Mother did not care to have him in the house. Gertrude bent and patted his head as she went past him, and the girls heard Grandma mention the ruts in the lane to Mother.

"There are always ruts after the thaw," said Mother. "John will see to them. Allie, put on the kettle."

"Let Gertrude put on the kettle," said Grandma. She beckoned to Allie to follow her into the parlor.

24

Suddenly Allie knew why Grandma had come, and she felt herself go stiff inside. She said nothing, however, but walked into the parlor. Her mother came after her and closed the door.

"I am told that Mary Alice has a pair of trousers," said Grandma.

Mother looked annoyed. "Who told you that?"

Grandma sat down in the rocker and folded her hands. "When I was a wee lass there was nothing I wanted more than to live on an island."

"I don't want to talk about it," said Mother.

"But I do," said Grandma. "Now why should Allie na' go with her father and at least see this island? And what an adventure it can be when she does!"

"But it's such nonsense!" cried Mother. "She'll never live there. It isn't even really ours. The whole idea of the trip is just a whim!"

"The world is made by whims, my girl, and don't you forget it," declared Grandma.

"It will serve no purpose," argued Mother.

"Must everything serve a purpose? What use is the moon? Come now, Ellen!"

Mother paused, and Allie knew that she was calling her arguments to mind.

"It's too cold," said Mother.

"If you wait until the summer, John will be too busy to take her. And if it's so cold, why do ye keep your windows open?"

"It's dangerous. She can't swim."

"John can swim, and Mary Alice is a sensible child. She'll not be leaping about in the dory."

"She can't go rigging herself up in trousers. I won't have it. What will people say?"

Gertrude opened the door to ask if they would have biscuits with the tea.

"Allie, go and help Gertrude," her mother ordered.

This time Grandma did not stop her. Allie went out, but she paused in the hall with Gertrude beside her.

"Mother, I will not be talked down in my own house," said Allie's mother. "She's only a child and she'll do as she's told."

"Aye, she is a child," said Grandma. "Your child, and John's too. Don't be selfish, Nell."

"Selfish? What has selfish to do with it?"

There was a hesitation in the parlor. Then Grandma said, "One would think you did na want to share the girls with John. Or is it your husband you do na want to share?"

Allie frowned.

"That's a terrible thing to say!" cried Mother.

"It is," said Grandma. "Well then, I'll not say it. If I thought such a thing, I'm mistaken, I'm sure."

"You certainly are!"

They neither of them said another word. Allie could hear Grandma's rocker squeak back and forth. She went on into the kitchen, where the kettle was boiling. Gertrude went with her and hovered between the stove and the door. "Mother sounds awfully cross. Do you think she'll let you go?"

26

"I don't know," said Allie. "It's . . . it's always so . . . such a business once she makes up her mind to something. I wish . . . I wish she was different."

"You're not supposed to wish that," said Gertrude quickly. "She's our mother!"

And that was true, but it did not keep Allie from feeling resentful. She said no more, however, but went on making the tea.

Three

That night Papa came home late from Guysborough. He paused in the kitchen doorway, so tall that his head almost touched the lintel, and he looked at Mother. His eyes were tense and watchful. Mother did not look at him, but only told him to get washed for dinner.

Dinner was silent, but when the last crumb had been eaten, and when Papa had announced that the apple cake was very good—even better than usual—Mother lowered her eyes to her hands. She made a motion as if she were smoothing the napkin on her lap. "If you are going off on this ridiculous expedition, the two of you, you had better look as respectable as we can manage. Allie, go and get those trousers and let me see them on you."

"Oh, good!" Gertrude jumped up and clapped. Mother turned her head as if she didn't want to notice.

Papa had left the trousers and the boots in the buggy.

He went out to get them, and Allie slipped out of her dress and pulled off her petticoat. When Papa was back, she sat down in her drawers to pull on the trousers. They were dark blue wool, heavy and rough, and they scratched. When she stood up she had to hold them to keep them from sliding down around her ankles.

"I'll take them in," said Mother.

"I should have bought a belt," remarked Papa.

"Why not a piece of rope?" Gertrude suggested.

"Because I would like her to look like a human being and not a ragamuffin," said Mother.

Allie sat down, feeling the bulk of the cloth between her legs. She wriggled.

"Don't do that!" snapped Mother. "Sit like a lady even if you aren't one! And don't think you'll wear those to drive to Canso, because you won't."

"No, Mother," said Allie, who did not care what she wore to Canso, so long as she got there.

"Are you going to stay overnight with Uncle Hugh?" asked Gertrude. "I like it at Uncle Hugh's. There's that covered walkway to the outhouse so you don't get cold when you have to go early in the morning."

"Gertrude, you aren't supposed to talk about such things," Mother scolded.

"But it's nice not to get cold," insisted Gertrude. "And I like it when Uncle Hugh shows us where John Paul Jones came in in 1776 and sank the fishing boats and then said he'd won a big battle."

"John Paul Jones was a pirate and a rebel," said Mother.

"I know. And we were loyal to good King George."

29

Papa laughed. "Gertrude, you weren't even an idea in the mind of God then. It was your great-great-grandfather who was loyal to King George."

"He lived in Connecticut," Gertrude continued, who loved the story, "and his neighbors didn't like him because he was loyal to the British, so he had to run away from his home in the middle of the night."

"With his gold sovereigns sewed into the bedquilts," said Allie, taking up the recital.

"And once his family was safe, he fought for the king," Gertrude added, "so the king gave us our land here because of what we lost in Connecticut."

"And we still have the land, and I'm glad," Allie finished the story. "I'm always going to live here."

"I'm not," said Gertrude. "When I'm grown I'll cut off my hair and ship out as a seaman, and I'll make lots of money and buy my own schooner." Gertrude had read *Treasure Island* after she finished *Robinson Crusoe* and had immediately decided that life as a seaman was to be preferred to anything more usual.

Mother only smiled. "If you cut your hair, perhaps you'll be able to keep it combed for a change."

Allie saw then that her mother's fit of pique had spent itself. The storm clouds had rolled by, and they could be comfortable again.

The next day was Wednesday, and when Allie and Gertrude came in from school Mother was ironing, and singing while she did that. Then it was Thursday, and on Thursday night after supper Papa brought the tub from the cellar and put it on the floor near the stove. He put a screen with wooden louvres around the tub and Allie had a bath. Her mother washed her hair. Then Allie sat next to the stove in her nightgown while Mother rolled the hair up on strips of rag so that it would be curly. Allie was to be very grand when she set out with her father on Friday.

"I don't know why I bother," said her mother. "You'll come home smelling like seaweed."

Allie slept fitfully on the rag curlers. On Friday morning she woke to a scramble and a hurry. Mother made her eat breakfast in her nightgown so that she would not get crumbs on any of her good clothes. Then she had to run upstairs and put on her best chemise, and the drawers of fine thin cotton, and a petticoat with a wide ruffle at the bottom. When she was ready, she called, and Mother came up to button her into her green silk dress.

When Mother finished the buttons, she brushed Allie's hair. It had not curled in spite of the rags. Allie's hair never curled. It was wavy, however, and it had a nice shine to it, with glints of red showing in the brown.

"Grandma's coming down the lane," Gertrude reported, looking out the window.

"At this hour?" Mother hurried down to the kitchen.

Allie put on her shoes and then took her bonnet from the shelf. It was made of the same silk as her dress and it had velvet ribbons.

"You look nice," Gertrude told her, when the bonnet was on.

Allie looked into the mirror. Her mouth was a bit too wide and her jaw was a bit too square. But she did look

31

nice in the green bonnet and the silk dress. "I'm not pretty, but I fix up well."

"That's almost as good," said Gertrude, who was pretty, with curly fair hair and a delicate, heart-shaped face.

The two went down then and found Grandma sitting near the stove. The visit was formal. Grandma was wearing the black silk apron which she usually put on in the afternoon. She had on the white woolen shawl with the fringe. It had been Grandpa's last gift to her, and Allie knew it was usually worn only on Sundays.

"Turn around and let me see you," said Grandma.

Allie turned.

"Very good."

Allie heard Papa's buggy stop at the gate. She picked up the satchel, which contained her nightgown and her other underthings and the much-disputed trousers. Mother went for Allie's coat, which was hanging on a peg in the hall. But the coat looked shabby when it went on over the green glimmer of the dress. Grandma gestured at Mother to take the coat away, and she took off her beautiful shawl and put it around Allie's shoulders.

"It looks well with that dress," said Grandma.

Allie touched it, and her fingers lingered. It was so soft. "But it's the shawl Grandpa bought for you. Suppose I get it dirty?"

"You won't. Go on now."

Papa was in the buggy. He took off his hat and bowed to Allie as if she were a grown lady. She grinned and climbed up to sit beside him. Gertrude handed up the satchel and the rubber boots. These went under the seat.

Then Mother handed up a basket with lunch in it, and Papa chirruped to Maude, and they were off.

Allie sat straight and proud, and tried not to bounce as the buggy rumbled and swayed over the ruts in the lane. Down past the sawmill they went. Mr. Kelly came out to wave, and then Allie heard someone shouting her name. It was Tom Anderson, running across the fields with his hat in his hand and his jacket only half buttoned.

"Allie, wait!"

Papa reined in the horse and Tom dashed up, red-faced from running. Allie saw that he hadn't stopped to comb his hair that morning.

"You're going to the island," he said. "Listen, have a good time."

"I will," she replied. She thought since he had been in such a rush to wish her well, she would ask politely what he would do that day. But before she could get the question out he had dug into his jacket pocket and brought out a little wooden object.

"Here." He handed the thing up to Allie. "I made this for you, in case you . . . you need one."

It was a whistle he had whittled. Allie turned it in her hand, seeing the hole in one end to blow into, and the notched opening halfway down where the air would whistle through.

Allie looked down at Tom, pleased that he had done this for her. She had no special need of a whistle, and she could not imagine that there would be anyone to hear her blow it on Papa's island, but it was good of him all the same. "Thank you," she said.

To her surprise, he turned red and lowered his head so that she could not see his eyes.

"Be careful," he warned.

"I will," Allie promised. Tom stepped away from the carriage, Papa clucked to the mare, and they were off once more.

Allie looked back. Tom was standing in the road looking after them, his legs spread so that he seemed solidly planted there, like some sort of tow-headed, stubby oak. He waved at her and she waved back.

"It's a very nice whistle," said Papa. "I used to make whistles like that when I was Tom's age—and sometimes I gave them to girls when I was sweet on them."

"Tom isn't sweet on me," said Allie. "He's just . . . just Tom."

Papa chuckled, and Allie bent and slipped the whistle into the lunch basket. She wondered about Tom. Could he be sweet on her? It seemed odd even to think of it. He was just Tom, and he sat next to her at school and drew pictures in his copybook when he should be studying. Twice a week he came to the house to carry wood and bring in water and scrub the kitchen floor. She had known him forever.

Then Allie stopped thinking about Tom, for they were on the road to Guysborough and she could see the bay, with the water cold and gray as steel and fog standing out on the horizon. "It won't rain, will it?" she asked.

"It wouldn't dare," said her father.

They went on through Guysborough, past Uncle Matt's store, which was not open yet, and before they were three miles on the Canso road the fog had wisped away and the sun had burned through the clouds. Allie let her grandmother's shawl drop back from her shoulders.

She loved the Canso road. There was always the sea to the left. Sometimes it whispered and sometimes it roared, depending on the day. Now it whispered. So did the pines beside the road. Now and then they saw a cottage that was silvered by sun and salt. Sometimes there was a little pier jutting out into the water with a dory bobbing beside it. Once Allie saw a fox scramble to get itself under cover before they could overtake it.

Late in the morning they stopped at Allie's favorite place. It was a stretch of clean sand between the road and the sea. Allie liked to sit there and feel the sun warm on her face and listen to the sound the waves made when they broke on the shore. She sat now and watched Papa take down the lunch basket and the lap robe that was always folded in the buggy. He spread the robe and opened the basket and said, "Cold chicken!"

"I know."

"And bread and butter and cake."

"I made the cake."

Papa bowed to her, a smile lifting the corners of his mustache. "You are becoming accomplished. Spread the napkin now, so you won't get anything on yourself. Elegance is a great responsibility."

Allie sighed. "I should have worn my school dress. Then I wouldn't have to worry."

"Your mother wouldn't like it. She wants you to make a good impression."

"On Uncle Hugh? Why? He's family."

"He's an important man in Canso, and your mother imagines half the people in the town watch to see who comes to visit him."

Allie knew that her mother felt this way. And she knew that some people might notice Uncle Hugh's coming and goings. Uncle Hugh worked at a bank, and he decided who might borrow money, and who could not borrow. He lived in a house that was big enough for a great family, but there were no children and there was no wife. There was only an Irish girl named Kathleen, who came in by the day to cook Uncle Hugh's meals and to keep him tidy.

"Why didn't Uncle Hugh get married?" Allie asked, thinking of that big house.

"He wanted to once," said Papa. "The girl was a beauty, but she wouldn't have him."

"Why not?"

"She thought his red hair was common."

"Common? How could she think that? It's what the Lord gave him."

Papa grinned. "Some people think the Lord doesn't always have good taste. Never mind. She must have been a witless one, and Hugh is better off without her."

They ate their lunch then, and Papa packed the basket and the robe back into the buggy, and they set off again. Sometimes the road ran along the cliffs, high above the water, and sometimes it dipped down to the level of the beach. Sometimes they could not see the sea at all for the woods that grew thick beside the road, but always they could feel it there like a great presence. Allie looked now and again to see if there might be a glimpse of an island far out there, yet she knew she was foolish for doing it. Their island had to be nearer to Canso.

As the day wore on Allie began to feel they had been on the Canso road forever, listening to the rhythm of Maude's hoofs. She caught herself nodding.

"Why don't you take off your bonnet and put your head down for a bit?" suggested her father.

She did, feeling the hardness of Papa's muscles under the trousers, and the warmth of Grandma's shawl which Papa spread over her, for the wind was fresh in spite of the sunshine. In a few minutes Allie was asleep. She did not wake until they were in Canso and her father was shaking her.

She sat up and saw Papa reining Maude in and Uncle Hugh hurrying out of his house to meet them. He went around the carriage to help Allie down. Kathleen came out, big-boned and red of wrist, to help carry in the things. Then Allie saw that there was someone else. A woman stood in the doorway of the house, watching them.

Four

When Allie got closer, she saw that the woman in the doorway was really only what Grandma would call a slip of a girl. True, her dress came to the floor, and her hair did not cascade down her back as Allie's did. It was worn in a high smooth roll that made her head look too big for the rest of her. Her waist was so small that Allie knew she must wear a corset. Just the same, there was a soft roundness to her face that made Allie think she was young—perhaps not yet twenty.

"Allie, this is Miss Jane Cameron," said Uncle Hugh. He smiled such a proud smile at Miss Cameron that Allie thought he might well have invented her.

Papa was presented to the lady, and she smiled and gave him her hand. Allie saw that her teeth were a bit too big for her face, and she found this defect strangely comforting.

"I'm pleased to meet you, Mr. Hughes," said Miss Cameron to Papa.

Papa went to put Maude in the stable behind the house, and Allie and Uncle Hugh trailed after Miss Cameron to the parlor. There sat a couple who turned out to be Miss Cameron's uncle and aunt.

Allie retreated a step when she was presented to the aunt, whose name also was Cameron. She was a broad woman with a ruddy face and quantities of very black hair. She had a great deal of bosom and resembled those ladies who were carved on the prows of ships. However, those ladies usually did not wear many clothes. Mrs. Cameron was thoroughly clothed, and everything she wore was ruffled or swirled or draped. Allie was suddenly afraid that Mrs. Cameron might attempt to hug her, and that she might smother in the ruffles.

Mrs. Cameron did not hug, but she put her hand to Allie's collar and to Allie's cheek. Allie knew then that she was a toucher, like Miss Atwater, a lady who lived in Guysborough. Allie had seen Miss Atwater in Uncle Matt's store, and she knew she always had to put her hands on a thing before she could believe it.

Mr. Cameron was quite unlike his wife. He was a stringy little man who looked as if he had been left out in the rain to shrink and fade. When Allie was presented to him he looked at her with watery eyes and said, "Um," and then he glanced at his wife as if hoping she would approve.

Papa came in and sent Allie upstairs to wash before dinner. Allie was glad enough to go up to the little blue room at the top of the stairs. She found Kathleen there putting coal on the fire.

"Who are those people downstairs?" she asked.

"The Camerons?" Kathleen poured water from the pitcher into the big china basin and began to undo the buttons at the back of Allie's dress. "They're from Dartmouth. Mr. Cameron has something to do with the ferry there. He buys and sells things."

"You mean he keeps a store?"

"Not exactly. It's some sort of big things he buys and sells. Boats. Or engines. I'm not sure. He's very important."

"He doesn't look important." Allie pulled the dress over her head.

Kathleen smiled. "Then she makes up for the two of them, doesn't she? And how do you like Miss Jane? Your uncle met her at church."

"She's . . . she's nice, I guess. Are they staying for dinner?"

"They are."

That was a bit of a disappointment. Allie had been looking forward to the dinner with Uncle Hugh, who always treated her like a grownup who should be listened to. Now it was Miss Jane Cameron who would be listened to.

Allie washed and Kathleen handed the towel to her so that she could wipe her face and hands. Then Kathleen buttoned her into her dress and Allie went out and down the stairs, hearing Mrs. Cameron's voice every step of the way. Mrs. Cameron was speaking of London.

"We were not presented to King Albert. He was in the

country. But the journey was inspiring just the same. London can seem like home to one who is well read. The Poets' Corner at Westminster Abbey keeps one engrossed for hours. And, of course, that grim old Tower. Such terrible things happened there, one can hardly bear to think of them."

Allie felt that it might be rather nice to scream, or to throw something at Mrs. Cameron. Of course she did neither. She set her teeth and walked into the parlor. Miss Jane smiled at her and moved to make room on the settee so that Allie could sit beside her. Allie sat, folding her hands in her lap, and Mrs. Cameron talked on. She described the trip across the English Channel to France, and Allie wondered if they would have a tour of all of Europe. But that was not to be, for Mrs. Cameron suddenly leaned toward Uncle Hugh and said, "Jane has had every advantage, as if she were our very own daughter. When she is older, perhaps she will appreciate the trouble we've been to."

Uncle Hugh blinked and said nothing, so Mrs. Cameron turned toward Papa. "Poor Jane. Her father was a charming man, but feckless. Never a care for the morrow. He was the one who insisted on that mad expedition."

"Expedition?" said Papa. Allie wondered if Miss Jane's father had hunted lions in Africa or shot tigers in India.

"A walk in the rain, if you please," said Mrs. Cameron. "In November. In Halifax."

"Oh," said Papa. He sounded disappointed.

"My poor sister-in-law. She always went along with him, whatever he said, poor moonstruck thing. They went

41

for their walk and got chilled through and were dead in no time. Galloping consumption, and poor Jane an orphan with no one to look after her but Mr. Cameron and myself."

Mrs. Cameron nodded then, glowing with virtue. "We took her and raised her like our own, and never a word of the trouble or expense. She's been brought up like a princess, and I know she's deeply grateful, though she doesn't say much."

Mrs. Cameron looked at Jane, and Allie thought the look was a reproach.

Jane was silent. Allie peeked at her sideways. She saw that Miss Jane Cameron had her head bowed, as if she found the pattern of the carpet interesting. But she was not looking at the carpet. She was looking at Uncle Hugh's feet. Across the room, Uncle Hugh was contentedly ignoring Mrs. Cameron and watching Miss Jane. Papa was watching Uncle Hugh. As for Mr. Cameron, he had fallen asleep.

Allie almost felt sorry for Mrs. Cameron. She was talking so energetically, and no one was listening. But during dinner Allie's sympathy vanished. Mrs. Cameron was never silent. Allie imagined her like some terrible talking machine, going night and day, never running down. No one else could utter a thought.

After dinner Papa announced that Allie would have to go to bed. "Tomorrow will be a long day," he said. He did not say why it would be a long day, and Allie guessed that he did not want to mention the trip to the island, lest

Mrs. Cameron predict a fit of galloping consumption for Allie.

Allie was grateful to Papa. "I'll ask Kathleen to undo my buttons."

"Don't ask Kathleen," said Miss Jane Cameron. "I'll help you."

She and Allie went up to the little blue room and Miss Jane undid the buttons. Allie took off her dress and hung it on a peg behind the door, and then she took her comb from the bureau. "Are you going to braid your hair?" Miss Jane asked.

"If I don't, it'll be all snarls in the morning."

"Let me do it."

"You don't have to," said Allie. "I do it all the time."

"But I'd like to," said Jane.

So Allie sat on the bed, and Jane sat beside her and combed and smoothed Allie's hair and then started on the braids. She did not talk. Allie thought she must be weary of talk and no wonder. "Is it hard for you sometimes?" Allie asked.

"Is what hard?"

"Being grateful." Allie looked around quickly, wondering if she had said too much. But Jane was not angry. She was staring past Allie at the lamp.

"They *are* very good to me."

Saying that did not seem to make Jane joyful, and Allie decided that Grandma must be right when she said that gratitude was not a natural virtue. She might also have said that those who demanded it seldom got more than an imitation of the real thing.

43

Jane finished the braids and stood up. She said goodnight and closed the door. Allie skinned out of her underthings into her nightgown and into bed, where she lay wondering.

It was plain to see that Uncle Hugh was greatly taken with Jane. Perhaps Jane was also taken with him, though she did no more about it than sit and stare at his shoes. Were they in love? And if they were, would Uncle Hugh face a lifetime filled with Mrs. Cameron and her talk?

Then Allie was glad that she was safe in bed, away from the torrent of words. She tried to imagine what tomorrow would be like, with just herself and Papa out on the broad ocean. And then she stopped her wondering, for she was asleep.

Five

The journey began in the shivering chill before dawn. It began with warnings.

"Now see that you're careful," said Kathleen.

"I will." Allie was as close to the kitchen stove as she could get. She hunched her shoulders, put her hands into the pockets of her new trousers, and watched Kathleen beat the oatmeal with a wooden spoon.

Uncle Hugh came in and Kathleen poured coffee for him. Allie carried it to him at the table.

"Um," said Uncle Hugh, who seldom spoke before nine.

Papa came in humming, pulling his sweater straight. He was taller than Uncle Hugh, and darker, and in the mornings he was brisk. "Good morning, Kathleen! Allie! Hugh!"

"Um," said Uncle Hugh.

Kathleen poured a second cup of coffee and Allie took

45

it to Papa. The eggs spluttered in the skillet, and Allie smelled the sharpness of bacon. Then everything was ready and they ate. By the time they finished the light from the lamp on the table was thin and the sun was up over the rim of the ocean.

"No fog this morning," said Papa. "Are you ready?"

Allie was ready, but Kathleen was not. The basket they had brought from home had to be packed with cold chicken and bread and butter. A tin of cookies went in, and a pie plate filled with cold slices from last night's roast.

"We're only staying the day," said Papa.

"The sea air makes you hungry," Kathleen told him.

Kathleen loved to say that. She had been born on a farm in Ireland and had lived all her life on the edge of a peat bog before she came to Nova Scotia. When she did come, the voyage to Halifax had been rough. Just the same, Allie had heard her boast that she had not had a minute sick. She was the only one aboard who never missed a meal, and she had not missed one since.

When even Kathleen was satisfied and the basket was closed, Allie and Papa set out for the pier. Uncle Hugh walked with them, drowsing as he went.

"Fine boy you've got there, Mr. Hughes," said the old man who tended to the boats at the pier.

"I've another one at home just waiting to grow into those britches," said Papa. "Allie's going to be bailer on this trip. Turn around, Allie, and show yourself to Mr. McIver."

Mr. McIver grinned at her when she turned, and nodded.

Then he busied himself opening the lock on the shed where the oars were kept. He took some time with it for the lock kept trying to slip away from the key. Papa pretended not to notice, and he did not try to help. Mr. McIver had been a fisherman until the day he tore his hand on a hook. The wound had been nothing. Allie knew that every fisherman on the coast had scarred hands. But for Mr. McIver, that one time, there had been no healing. The cut had festered and the flesh around it had gone ugly. Red streaks had appeared on Mr. McIver's arm. Now McIver did not row a dory. Only a man with two hands can row a dory.

When the shed was open, McIver handed a pair of oars out to Papa. Allie saw that Papa's initials, JCH, were neatly cut into the wood just above the blades.

Mr. McIver had a little tin bucket which Allie could use to bail. Last to come out of the shed was the box with Papa's tools.

Then there were warnings again.

"Mind yourself, lass," said Mr. McIver.

"Be careful," said Uncle Hugh, and that was a great sentence for him to utter so early in the day.

Papa climbed down the ladder to the dory. Hugh handed down the tools and the lunch, and these went on the seat in front and were lashed in place. Then Allie went down the ladder and she went on the seat in the back. Papa sat in the middle and Mr. McIver untied the dory. Papa pushed against a piling with an oar and they were off.

Papa rowed easily, his feet braced against the sides of the boat. Allie dabbled her boots in the water in the bottom of the boat, then looked back at the pier. Mr.

McIver waved, but Uncle Hugh did not stir. "I think Uncle Hugh's asleep," said Allie.

"He'll wake up in time," said Papa. "Start bailing. You've got to earn your keep."

Allie bailed, scooping splintery water out of the boat with the bucket Mr. McIver had given her. Papa's oars dipped into the water, pulled, then lifted. The dory passed the fishing boats that were moored in the harbor, then cleared the harbor. They rode up a long, smooth swell, then slid down the other side.

Allie felt a strangeness in her stomach. She had not expected this, and it surprised her. All her life she had lived close to the sea, lingering sometimes on the bluffs above the docks in Guysborough. She had seen the fishermen with their hands roughened from the wet and the weather, and their throats hoarse as if the fog had become part of them. Yet she had seldom really been on the water. She did not swim and her mother was fearful. Besides, it was not proper for a girl to scramble about in a boat, at least if one listened to Mother.

Now she was doing it, and now there was the open water between herself and Papa's island. It had to be crossed, and Allie wondered if she could do it.

Papa said, "Lean into it, Allie," and the next swell was coming toward them.

Allie leaned forward. She fixed her eyes on the top of the watery slope. For an instant she saw the wave green and glowing with sunlight. Then it was beneath them and Allie could not see it. She leaned back as they sped down into the trough.

Allie's breakfast decided to stay where it belonged. Allie smiled a quick smile so that Papa would know she was all right. She bailed again.

After a while she looked back to see Canso small behind them. She could see the dock, but Mr. McIver was not there, and neither was Uncle Hugh. The houses in the town were toy houses marching up the hill away from the water.

There was a swell that Allie did not see because she was looking back. She felt the dory lift and she turned to see the green-gold sea. Then the swell was under them and they dropped again into the trough.

For a terrifying moment Allie wondered whether the water was not seeping into the boat faster than she could ladle it out. She bent to her bailing.

Soon Papa said, "You can rest now, Allie. Don't worry. There's always a little water in a dory."

Allie rested, looking up and seeing a gull riding the blue wind above them. The gull had something in its beak.

"He's got a herring," said Papa. "That's a good sign."

"Why?" she asked.

"Where there's herring, there's cod. The fishermen will follow the gulls for miles to find the cod."

The gull dipped away behind them, and Allie bailed again. Then she rested and then bailed. When it seemed that they had been a long, long time on the ocean, Allie saw an island off to the left.

"Is that it?"

"No, not yet."

On they went, and there was another island. Papa looked

over his shoulder, pulled on an oar to change course a bit, and then they were in smooth water in the lee of the island. The sea swells were gone.

"Is it ours?" asked Allie.

"It's ours."

Allie looked up. The cliffs were sun white and salt white and crowned with oaks. Below the cliffs there was a beach where the sand was golden. Allie saw shacks beyond the beach, unpainted, boarded up now so that they had an abandoned look. She saw a little dock that ran out to the deep water. Papa brought them in close to this dock and reached out to hold the ladder that was nailed to one of the pilings.

"Up you go now," he said to Allie.

Allie went crouching to grasp the ladder, holding to the side of the boat as she went. She climbed up to the dock and Papa threw her the rope from the boat, which she wrapped around the top of a piling to make the boat fast. Papa passed up the tool box and the lunch basket, then came up the ladder himself.

Allie turned and saw a path at the end of the dock. Beyond the dock, pulled up on the beach, there was a dory.

"Someone's here," she said. Her voice was flat. She had not expected this. She had thought she would have the day alone with Papa.

Papa nodded. "It belongs to Mr. MacManus, I'm sure. He comes every spring to keep up the grave."

"A grave? You never said there was a grave here." Allie

felt herself shiver. Somehow it was eerie to think of a grave on Papa's island.

"It's on top of the cliffs. Mr. MacManus tends it because he thinks his sweetheart may be buried there."

"He thinks? Doesn't he know?"

"No one knows for sure. Mr. MacManus came from Ireland when he was very young. He took to farming and did well at it, and as soon as he felt he was ready, he sent for the girl who had promised to come after him. She set out, and he went to Halifax to meet her ship. It never came in."

"It sank?"

"With all on board," said Papa. "Near that time the body of a woman was carried in here on the tide. A fisherman lived on the island then—a sort of hermit who tended his lines and kept to himself. He found the woman on the beach and he did the best he could for her. He sewed her body into a sail and buried her on the bluff, and he marked the place with an oar. Later, when he went to Canso to get supplies, he told the story. It reached MacManus and he decided that the woman must be his Mary. Ever since, he comes here in the spring."

Papa pointed to a path that led up to the cliffs. "We'll say good day to him. He's a fine man."

They climbed, with Allie stretching to match her father's stride. The path underfoot was sun-bleached and clean, like the beach below. Allie knew from things her father had said that as the season went on, this would change. The fishermen would come and there would be the stink of cod drying in the open sheds and the smell of fires built to warm the shacks where the men slept. But now there was the sun, the clean wind, and the new grass growing beside the path, and herself and her father.

And Mr. MacManus.

They saw him as soon as they reached the top of the bluffs. He was there kneeling beside a pile of stones, a paintbrush in his hand. He turned his head toward them and nodded. "Mr. Hughes," he said. "Fine day."

"Mr. MacManus," said Papa, "will you meet my daughter."

MacManus put the paintbrush down across the top of the whitewash bucket and stood, wiping his hands on the legs of his trousers.

"This is Allie," said Papa.

MacManus bowed and his eyes crinkled. Allie was surprised. She had expected to see a man aged and worn with grief. Mr. MacManus looked weathered, but so did most men who worked out in the wind and the weather. His hair was scarcely touched with gray, and his eyes were an intense blue.

"You favor your father, I think," said MacManus to Allie.

"So they say," agreed Papa. "Allie's come to explore our island. We'll have our lunch later in the grove near the spring. We'd be pleased if you'd join us."

MacManus nodded and went back to his work. Half the pile of stones gleamed white and half were gray and dull. There was no oar to mark the grave now. Instead there was a wooden cross. It was gray too, from the snow and the sun, but Allie could read the lettering on it: Mary Delehanty, 1872–1891.

"I'll give you a shout when we're ready," Papa promised. Then he and Allie went back down to the beach.

"His Mary was very young," said Allie. "Only nineteen." She felt solemn. Nineteen was not that much older than twelve. "Do you think it really *is* his Mary buried there?"

"It comforts him to think so," Papa answered. "When we have our lunch he will tell us how lovely she was, and that comforts him too."

Allie felt that if she had heard this story in her mother's parlor she would have thought it very sad. Somehow it was not so sad here on the island. Mr. MacManus had his comfort, and his Mary would always be lovely and would never grow old and stout and perhaps short of temper.

"I like it here," said Allie.

Papa smiled. "I knew you would."

He set to work then. For a while Allie watched, and when she had a chance she helped. She handed nails to Papa and held his tools, and one after another the shacks along the shore were opened, and the roofs were looked at to be sure they were tight, and Papa checked the walls to make sure there were no chinks. Even in summer the wind could be cold. Each shack had a little stove, and Papa examined the stovepipes and looked at the grates.

Papa did not talk much while he worked, and Allie tried to imagine what it would be like to live on the island. It would be hard, she knew, for everything that was needed would have to be brought in a boat. Still, it would be an adventure, and there might be a sort of joy in it. As Papa said, on the island you could imagine you were king of the world.

Allie was pondering this interesting idea when Papa declared that it was lunchtime. She realized all of a sudden that she was very hungry. She ran to get the basket, and she and Papa set out for the top of the island. When they passed Mr. MacManus, Papa called to him. He came after them with his own lunch wrapped in a napkin. They kept walking until they came to a place where oak trees grew close to a little stream that bubbled from the earth. They sat there, with the trees giving them some shelter from the wind, and Papa opened the basket.

Mr. MacManus had bread and meat and an apple. Allie and Papa shared their cookies with him, and he spoke of his lovely Mary, as Papa had predicted.

"She used to sing," said MacManus. "I remember sitting in her mother's kitchen watching her clear away the dishes, and she was singing the old songs. It was a miracle what a sweet voice she had. I'll hear it again one day, for they say that in heaven you'll know your own. In the meanwhile, the Lord must be enjoying it, for it was He who made her to sing."

Allie thought that if Mr. MacManus was mourning, he was doing it in as pleasant a way as anyone could.

"It's a wonder the things the Lord has done for us here and hereafter," said Mr. MacManus. "We've not found out the half of them, I'm sure."

Allie nodded. "He made the world and everything in it."

"Yes, and what tricks He played and what fun He must have had."

"Tricks?" Allie always thought of the Almighty as being very solemn.

"Have you never seen a camel?" said Mr. MacManus.

Allie hadn't, but she had seen pictures.

"Imagine thinking of a thing like a camel!" said MacManus. "Or a giraffe! Now there's a joke for you. And take that spring we're sitting by. Where do you suppose the water comes from?"

"It comes out of the ground," said Allie.

"And before that?"

"I suppose the rain makes it."

Papa smiled. "It never runs dry, Allie. Taste it."

She tasted. The water was fresh.

"Do you think it rains that much?" asked Papa.

"Well, then, where does it come from?" Allie wanted to know.

"That's one of the tricks," said MacManus. "It must come from the ocean. But how does seawater seep up through the rocks and sand and purify itself so that it runs fresh? I don't understand it, but I am sure the Lord does, and it's a clever thing, however it's managed."

They had finished their lunch. Papa gathered things and put them back into the basket, and Mr. MacManus folded his napkin, crumbs and all, and tucked it into his pocket. Then, since Mr. MacManus had finished his work on the grave, the three of them walked together down to the beach. Papa went to work mending the roof on one of the shacks, and Mr. MacManus stood by to help him. Allie was left to herself.

She put the basket down at the end of the dock, and opened it for a moment. Tom's whistle was there, together with crumpled napkins and the other debris of lunch. She took it out and blew a short little blast. The thing had a thin, shrill sound, and when Allie looked around she saw that her father had stopped his work for a moment and was watching her. She thought of Tom, standing in the lane giving her the whistle. Papa had said he was sweet on her. Allie felt herself blush. She put the whistle back in the basket, then wandered off along the beach.

Now and then she waded out a few feet. Here on the lee side of the island, the waves were no more than ripples, but Allie could feel the coldness of the water pressing on the outside of her boots. Sometimes she stooped to pick up a stone to take back to Gertrude, who liked stones. The water had no color at all when she looked down at it, but when she looked out away from the beach it was very blue, with not a cloud anywhere. Allie imagined that she could see the curve that was the shape of the earth out there where the sky and the sea met.

When the pockets of her trousers bulged with stones, she went back to the dock. Her father was wandering among the shacks, testing doors and looking up at roofs. Mr. MacManus was on the dock, his hands in his pockets. He was looking out over the water, and Allie went to stand beside him.

"Beautiful, is it not?" said MacManus. "A wonder. But not one of the jokes. I have seen it cruel."

Allie thought of the grave on the bluffs. She said nothing, and he looked down at her and smiled. "Come now, not so serious."

He started to turn about, his hands still in his pockets, and Allie saw it begin to happen before even he knew it was happening. There was a wide crack between two of the planks in the dock, and when he turned MacManus caught the edge of his boot in that crack. He tried to take a step, and he stumbled sideways and began to fall.

Allie saw his blue eyes go wide with surprise, and he kept falling and falling. It took so long for him to fall away from her, silent, shocked, struggling to get his hands out of his pockets, she thought he would never be done with it. But at last the falling was over and there was a splash.

"Papa!" Allie screamed.

MacManus was in the water, and now his hands were free, but they beat uselessly at the surface. He was not a yard from the ladder, yet he beat at the water and stared up with terrible, wide-eyed surprise. Then the water was over his face and Allie could not see his eyes.

"Papa, he can't swim!" Allie screamed.

MacManus surfaced.

"The ladder!" Allie shouted. "Grab the ladder!"

He did not hear. He struggled and he did not hear.

Afterward Allie did not remember doing it. She only remembered being at the bottom of the ladder with her feet in the water. She stretched one leg to MacManus, and his hands clutched at her ankle. Then her boot slipped off and he was clutching again, holding fast to her foot.

That was enough. Allie waited, holding the ladder, not speaking, and then Papa was beside her and behind her, putting himself between her and the sea. He held the ladder with one hand, and with the other he reached down to take MacManus by the wrist.

"I have you," said Papa to MacManus. "Let go of her."

MacManus let go.

Allie went up the ladder and stood trembling on the dock. She watched Papa get MacManus's hands onto the ladder and then fairly drag him out, scrabbling and gasping, and boost him up the ladder to the dock.

MacManus stretched out flat, his face against the splintery planks. Papa stood and put his arms around Allie. She hugged him and felt that he was shaking. Or was it herself that was shaking?

"You're the bravest lass I ever knew, and thank God you didn't jump in to save him!"

"But Papa, I can't swim either."

He tried to laugh, but he choked on it. "For a second I was afraid that wasn't going to stop you."

Six

Papa built a fire on the beach, and Mr. MacManus dried himself before the flames, turning this way and that with the clothes still on him. After that there was the long pull back to Canso, with MacManus laboring along in Papa's wake.

Allie sat with her foot wrapped in an old oilskin slicker that Papa had found in one of the sheds. She bailed and watched MacManus struggle with his oars. Again and again she seemed to see his face staring up at her, then the water closing over him. What if Papa had not been there? Would MacManus have slipped away, lost in the sea like his Mary? Or would he at last have reached out to grasp the ladder?

Allie shivered, feeling herself very small and weak, and the sea around her very large.

The first lights were showing in the town when they

reached Canso. Uncle Hugh was waiting on the dock, and so was Mr. McIver.

"You've made a day of it," said Uncle Hugh, who was never sleepy at night.

"Everything all right, Mr. Hughes?" Mr. McIver looked down at Allie. "What's wrong with your foot, lass?"

Allie opened her mouth to answer, but Papa spoke first. "She waded off the beach and lost a boot. It's no great matter."

Allie closed her mouth. Papa had told a lie and had done it as easily as he breathed. She held her tongue and climbed the ladder to the dock, knowing that Papa doubtless had good reasons if he wanted to keep Mr. McIver from knowing what had really happened.

Papa made his dory fast, then turned to help MacManus.

"I'm much obliged to you, Mr. Hughes," said Mac-Manus. Allie thought that perhaps he meant more by it than he cared to say at the moment.

"No trouble, Mr. MacManus," said Papa.

"And I'm sorry about your boot," said MacManus to Allie.

Allie wanted to say it wasn't important, but she thought of Mother. What would Mother say when she heard about MacManus and his fall off the dock? And about Allie's part in the rescue? She would scold. She would declare that Allie might have drowned, and she would say that that's what came of letting a girl go off to the ends of the earth in a small boat. She would say it would be tempting providence for Allie to go ever again. And when it was Gertrude's turn, Gertrude would not go.

Allie looked down at her bare foot and decided that Gertrude would never forgive her.

"There's little use in one boot, is there?" remarked Mr. MacManus. "Perhaps you'd not mind letting me have that one you have on? It will be something to help me remember the day."

Allie thought that if she were MacManus, she would not be quick to forget the day. Still, if he wanted the boot he could have it. She sat down on the dock, pulled it off, and handed it to him. For an instant she thought that perhaps he planned to get her another pair. But it was late, and the shops were closed, and tomorrow was Sunday.

MacManus thanked her and walked away down the pier.

Mr. McIver looked after him. "That one looks as if he's been in the sea."

Papa did not comment, but only handed his oars to McIver. Then he and Uncle Hugh and Allie started away. Allie had stuffed her socks into her pocket, so she limped along on her bare feet. When they were out of earshot of McIver, Uncle Hugh said, "Don't tell me Allie lost her boot when she was wading. It's something to do with MacManus, isn't it?"

"He fell off the pier," explained Papa. "He panicked. Can't swim a stroke. Allie went down the ladder and stuck out her foot so he could hang onto it, and her boot came off."

"Well now!" said Uncle Hugh. He grinned and thumped Allie on the back as if she were a big rough man. "You're the one now, aren't you?"

"Papa pulled Mr. MacManus out," said Allie. But she was pleased with the admiration.

That night they ate in the kitchen. Allie sat in her nightgown, and, because Mrs. Cameron was not there to weary them with her talk, Kathleen sat with them.

"What will we tell Mother about the boots?" said Allie. "Can we say I forgot and left them here?"

Uncle Hugh looked surprised, and Papa scowled. "*You* will say nothing at all," he told her. "If you start lying to your mother, God knows where it will end. Besides, you'd never get away with it. She'd know in a second you were lying."

"You lied to Mr. McIver!" said Allie, and then she quickly wished she hadn't, for it was rude, and the last thing in the world she wanted was to be rude to Papa.

"I embroidered a story a bit to save a good man some embarrassment," said Papa. "There is no law that says I must tell everyone everything they think they should know. When you have more experience in the world you may decide now and then that a bit of embroidery is in order. Until then, you'd be well advised either to tell the truth or to hold your tongue."

Papa seldom spoke so sternly to Allie, and she feared she might cry if she tried to answer.

"There now!" said Papa. "It's all right. I'll not make a liar out of either of us. Even if tomorrow is Sunday, I can go around early and haul old man Hennessy out of bed and have him open his shop for a few minutes before he goes off for the day. You'll have a new pair of boots before we get home, and then all you have to do is hold your tongue. There won't be any questions, so you won't have to give any answers."

"Yes, Papa," said Allie. She sounded so downcast that Kathleen cut an extra piece of currant cake for her. Kathleen believed in food as a cure for almost anything.

After dinner Allie was drowsing in a chair in the parlor while Uncle Hugh paced and smoked his pipe. He happened to stop at the window and look out onto the street. "I do believe," said Uncle Hugh, "that the boots are coming now."

Allie came wide awake. She ran to the window. There was Mr. MacManus coming along with a package under his arm. She started to rush to the door but then realized she was wearing her nightgown. She rushed to the stairs instead and went up two at a time.

Grandma's shawl was neatly folded on the seat of a chair in the blue room. Allie snatched it up, wrapped herself in it, and started back down the stairs. Mr. MacManus was in the hall, bowing to Kathleen as he took off his cap. When he saw Allie on the stairs he bowed to her. Kathleen stood like a statue with the door open and the night breeze stirring her skirts.

Papa came to the parlor door. He saw Kathleen and he saw Mr. MacManus, and the expression on his face was half a frown and half a smile, as if he was amused and waiting to see what would happen next.

"Kathleen!" he said at last.

Kathleen started.

"This is Mr. MacManus."

Kathleen closed the door, which was a good thing, for the night was chilly.

"I've brought boots for Allie," Mr. MacManus explained. "They're like the others. There's no difference at all." He handed the package to Allie. "We'd not want to upset your mother."

So he had guessed. And he had guessed there was not time to dawdle about the boots. Allie beamed.

Kathleen blurted out something about tea and plunged back into the kitchen.

"You will stay and have a cup to tea, I hope," said Papa to Mr. MacManus.

"Tea?" Then before Mr. MacManus could say more, Uncle Hugh came into the hall to shake his hand, and he was being ushered into the parlor.

Allie went to the kitchen and saw that the kettle was on the stove, though Kathleen was scarcely through washing up after dinner. Allie sat down and opened Mr. MacManus's parcel. The boots were perfect—shiny black, with a red band around the top. "Mother will never guess," she said happily.

Kathleen did not seem to hear her. She was getting the big tray down from the top of the cupboard. She clattered cups and saucers onto it and cut what was left of the cake into slices. Then she scooped sugar into the best sugar bowl. "I wonder if that man has had his supper yet," she said. "Perhaps I'd best cut a slice or two of the beef. Allie, look in the pantry and see if there are any mustard pickles left. If he's not had his supper, mustard pickles go well with beef."

Allie went for the pickles, and Kathleen sliced the bread and buttered it. She scalded the teapot and made the tea strong and black. When everything was ready, Allie held the door open so that Kathleen could carry in the tray.

She trailed Kathleen to the parlor, feeling a bit anxious. Mr. MacManus had probably expected a simple cup of tea and a biscuit to go with it. Kathleen was giving him a feast!

Allie sat beside Papa and watched Kathleen pour. The color was high in Kathleen's cheeks, and she glanced at Mr. MacManus from under her lashes as if she did not want him to know she was looking. Allie thought of Miss Jane Cameron watching Uncle Hugh's feet, and she understood what Kathleen was about. Kathleen was like Grandma. She had been struck by love the way some people were struck by thunderbolts or runaway horses.

Mr. MacManus ate all the roast beef on his plate and the pickles too. He had three slices of bread and butter and two pieces of cake. Between bites he kept saying that everything was good—very good. "A fine tea," he announced when he had finished. "I haven't had such a fine tea for many a day."

Kathleen murmered something that Allie did not hear, then took Mr. MacManus's plate from him. She sat with the plate in her hands and her eyes on the teapot.

Uncle Hugh got up. "I promised Ted Hawkins I'd stop in to see him tonight." He took his hat and went out.

"Allie, it's time you were in bed," said Papa. He waited while Allie got out of her chair, and then he went up the stairs with her.

"It was a wonderful day, Papa," she said, when they reached the upstairs hall. "Thank you."

Papa smiled. "Thank *you*!" Then he went into his room and shut the door.

Allie waited for a moment, hearing Mr. MacManus talk on in the parlor below. He was telling Kathleen about his farm. Allie wished that he would tell her about the spring of fresh water instead, and the other tricks that the Lord played. But then, Kathleen seemed greatly taken with him no matter what he talked about.

Allie went into her room and shut the door. She knelt to her prayers, and suddenly she saw Mr. MacManus in the water again, staring up at her in that terrible, unseeing way. His day at the island had nearly cost him his life, and now he sat with Kathleen, as contented as if there had been no terror. Had he thought of his Mary at all that evening? Perhaps not. Perhaps the Lord had taken a hand and sent Mr. MacManus to Kathleen so that he could forget Mary at last and get on with his life.

Allie got into bed and lay listening to the voices from downstairs. She closed her eyes and felt the bed move under her as the dory had moved that day. She was on the bluffs, listening to Mr. MacManus, and then she drifted away and was asleep.

Seven

When Allie and Papa drove up the lane on Sunday evening, Mother and Grandma were waiting at the gate. Gertrude was with them, and she fairly danced in her eagerness to hear about Allie's adventure.

"My word!" said Papa. "What a reception! Well, we know that they missed us."

He reined Maude in and Allie got down. Shep came running to jump up on her. Allie quickly took off Grandma's shawl before the dog could do it harm. She gave it to Grandma, who folded it over her arm and then kissed Allie.

"You're home safe at least," said Mother. She said it rather as if she had not expected it to turn out that way. She was still at the gate, and when Papa got down and went to kiss her, she hardly seemed to notice.

"Come tomorrow, Allie, and tell me everything," said

Grandma. She kissed Allie again and went up the lane with Shep trailing her like a faithful shadow.

"Did you walk all around the island?" Gertrude took hold of Allie's arm. "Was it wonderful? Did you fish?"

"Gertrude, come and fill the water glasses," said Mother. "Supper is almost ready. Allie, run and change your dress. If you get a spot on that silk it will be the very devil to get out."

Allie went in and Gertrude scampered after her halfway up the stairs. "Were there any fishermen there?" said Gertrude.

Allie heard Mother come into the kitchen. She heard something thump down hard on the table. "Gertrude!" called Mother. "I want you to fill the water glasses and I want you to fill them *now!*"

Gertrude scooted back down to the kitchen, and Allie went on up and changed her dress. There would be little talk of the island that night, thought Allie. She had gone and Mother had been gracious enough about it at the end. Now Mother wanted to hear no more about it. And no wonder, for even at the best of times Mother disliked the thought of the island. The care of it took Papa away so often.

That night, when the stones Allie had brought for Gertrude were set out in a row on the windowsill, Gertrude and Allie talked at last. The talk was in whispers as they lay in the darkness. "It was beautiful on the island," said Allie. She paused, hoping she could tell about it so that Gertrude would understand. She wanted Gertrude to feel how the sea was suddenly calm when the dory came into the lee of the island. She wanted to tell about the trees that grew on the bluffs, and how they were so very green against the blue sky. She wanted to describe the scoured whiteness of the cliffs.

"On the top of the cliffs there are oak trees," she began. That didn't really explain it, but it was the best she could do. "You have to climb a steep path to get up there, and once you get to the top the wind is loud and it pushes at you. And there's a grave."

She had not planned to mention the grave so quickly, but the instant she spoke of it Gertrude had to hear all about it. Allie told her about the poor lost Mary, and about Mr. MacManus coming to tend the grave. And that led Allie to speak of the magical spring where the water ran fresh, and of the way Mr. MacManus called it one of the Lord's tricks. She thought it wiser not to tell about Mr. MacManus falling into the sea. Gertrude often spoke without thinking, and it was best not to chance Mother finding out.

The thought of Mr. MacManus and the spring put Allie in mind of Mr. MacManus and Kathleen sitting with the tea tray between them, so she told Gertrude about that. "Now that Mr. MacManus has met Kathleen, perhaps he won't keep going to the island to tend the grave," said Allie. "He may decide to forget his Mary at last."

Gertrude didn't reply to that, for she was asleep. Soon Allie slept too, and when she woke it was broad daylight. Papa and Mother were talking in the kitchen below, and then Allie heard Papa go out.

Allie dressed and started down. When she was still on

the stairs, Papa's carriage rattled away down the lane, and when she went into the kitchen, she saw that Mother was cross. The corners of her mouth were pulled down.

"Your father has lost his mind," said Mother.

Allie said nothing, but went to the stove to get her oatmeal.

"He's hardly set foot in the house and now he's off again. This time it's to Halifax. There'll be more horses, and he's getting a man to take care of them. If he'd stay at home and tend to affairs here, we wouldn't need a man. Allie, don't keep poking at that oatmeal. Either take some or leave it alone."

Allie took some and sat down.

"Your father should be at the sawmill today, going over the accounts with Mr. Kelly. I know there must be money due us, and Kelly's a poor hand at collecting bills. And your father will be borrowing to buy the horses, or I miss my guess. It will be the mercy of God if we don't wind up in the poorhouse."

Allie did not smile, since a smile would only enrage Mother, but she was sure they would not find themselves in the poorhouse. Papa would collect any accounts that were due for the sawmill. Somehow, though he always had a new venture to think of, he managed the old. He collected the accounts and he talked to the landowners who might have timber to sell. He knew who in the county considered building, so the mill was always busy. Allie was glad, not only because of the money, but because she liked to hear the high singing of the saw as it cut through the wood. She liked the smell of the place too, with the piles of sawdust everywhere.

Papa had always seen that the sawmill was busy, and that it paid. Even when he was first arranging the lease on the island, and had had to spend days and days in Halifax, the sawmill had taken in the logs and put out the lumber— and the accounts had been settled. Things were easier for Papa now. He was in Canso only two or three days out of seven, but now there was the mare to think of, and soon there would be more horses. Then there would be the colts, and they would have to be trained. Allie never doubted that Papa would have the finest carriage horses in the province. And she never doubted that once he had mastered the business of horse breeding, he would go on to something else. That could be why he was hiring the man now to see to the horses. Perhaps he was already thinking of a new venture.

Gertrude came downstairs and went to Allie to have her dress buttoned. Then she spooned out a bowl of oatmeal and ate it. After a scramble to find her books, which were in the parlor, she and Allie went off down the lane, leaving Mother to her worries. Allie was sorry about the worries, but perhaps they were to be expected. Mother had grown up being poor and pinched, and that must leave a mark on a person. It could be like a broken bone that had mended but that still ached when the weather turned damp. Once you were poor, there might always be a part of you that feared it would happen again.

When they reached the schoolyard, Tom was waiting to hear about the island. He listened, his hands busy with whittling and the sun bright on his hair. He nodded as Allie spoke, and now and then he asked a question, and what he thought was marvelous was not the spring with the fresh water, or the oaks on top of the bluffs. He thought it was marvelous that Papa had put wire mesh on the sides of the drying sheds so that the seabirds could not steal the fish.

"Or the rats," he said. "I suppose there are rats!"

Allie shuddered. She had not seen a rat, and she did not want to believe there were any. Papa's island was too beautiful a place for rats, and it was horrid of Tom to have thought of them. She would have said so, but Mr. Blanchard rang the school bell, and they had to go in.

That afternoon when Allie and Gertrude got home, Mother and Mrs. Anderson were coming from the barn. They both looked weary, with their shoulders drooping and their hair wisping out from under the towels they had pinned on to protect themselves. Mother had a pail and a mop and Mrs. Anderson had a broom. And Mrs. Anderson was scolding—a thing Mrs. Anderson did very will.

"If it were my husband," she was saying, "he'd see to his horses himself. It's nonsense, that's what it is, and I wouldn't have it, not for a minute!" She took herself off across the fields without bothering to say a word to Allie and Gertrude.

Mother put the bucket down in the lane. "I've fixed a place in the barn where the hired man can stay. If we're to have one about the place, he has to sleep somewhere. Allie, go and see if I've forgotten anything. Mrs. Anderson talks so that I never know whether it's on my head or my heels I'm standing after she's been here."

Allie went into the barn, and Gertrude after her. They stood smelling the thick smell of hay and manure and leather, and looking into the big stall in the corner. It had been swept and scrubbed as clean as any room. The narrow bed from the smallest room in Grandma's house had been put up and neatly made. There was a chest of drawers that had been in the attic since Allie could remember, and a straight chair from the kitchen. It all looked snug and tight, like the picture of the ship's cabin in Gertrude's copy of *Treasure Island*.

Mother had come in behind the girls. "Well? What do you think!"

"It's wonderful!" cried Gertrude. "Can I sleep out here until the man gets here?"

"Certainly not. Here. Take the mop to the kitchen. And the bucket too. I left it in the lane."

Gertrude went with the mop over her shoulder like a soldier's rifle.

"It's nice, Mother," Allie said.

Mother nodded. "Perhaps it's a good thing we're to have a man about the place. Your father is away too often, and it's such a business to get Ted Anderson or Tom to come. And the stalls have to be mucked out no matter what."

Allie knew then that her mother had stopped objecting to the idea of a hired man. Indeed, she was almost looking forward to his arrival.

She had three days to wait before Papa came home. He

had not bought any horses, for the ones he had seen in Halifax had not pleased him, but the hired man was in the buggy. He was a black man, and when he got down from the buggy and took off his hat, Allie saw that his curly black hair had a bit of white over the ears. The man was not very young, even if there were no wrinkles in his dark face.

"This is Joe Johnson," said Papa. The man bowed to Mother and smiled. His teeth were very white.

"I fixed a place for you in the barn," said Mother.

"Thank you, ma'am." Joe Johnson's voice was soft, and he slurred his words together when he said, "I hope you hain't been to too much trouble on my account."

"No trouble at all," Mother said, and that was a gracious lie.

Joe Johnson ate with the family that night, sitting with his eyes on his plate and his knife in his left hand. He used the knife to push food onto the back of his fork, and as he carried the food to his mouth he bent forward and did not sit straight as Mother insisted everyone must.

"Why do you do that with your knife?" Gertrude asked after a while.

"Gertrude!" Mother's tone was a warning.

Joe was not offended. "It be handy this way. I wouldn't want none of this good dinner to get away from me."

Papa chuckled.

Gertrude was still for a breath or two, then said, "What did you do in Halifax? Did you take care of horses there too?"

"Yes, ma'am. I was workin' in a livery stable when I

74

met your daddy, and he said he reckoned I'd be more satisfied here."

"Gertrude, eat your supper and let Joe eat his," said Papa. "Joe is from the United States—from Kentucky, where they breed splendid horses. He's going to be a huge help to me, but it would be nice if he could have a meal in peace before he starts."

Gertrude was quiet then, but she kept watching Joe. When he finished eating he thanked Mother and said he had had a wonderful meal. Then he retreated to the barn.

In a day or two it seemed that Joe had always been there. Papa bought a stove in Guysborough to keep his place in the barn warm. Soon Joe was taking his meals there, carrying a tray out from the kitchen. He was up early every day, quietly doing things that needed doing. He put up extra shelves in the corner of the cellar where the preserves were kept. He spaded the earth for Mother's kitchen garden. He split wood and built fires. Of course he mucked out the stalls, and after ten days there was more of that sort of thing to do. Papa came home from Antigonish with two more mares.

With Joe so willing, there was less and less for Tom Anderson to do. At first Allie was afraid he would simply stay away. He did not. He took to arriving even when he wasn't sent for, and he would lean on the fence, whittling and watching Sissy. The mare was almost ready to have her foal, and now that the brief springtime was passing and the days were warmer, Joe turned her out to the pasture every day. Sissy stood there seeming to gaze off into the distance. Now and then she munched on the grass that grew green and long at her feet, or turned her head as if listening to something no one else could hear. Allie thought she looked heavy and clumsy, with her sides round as a barrel.

Joe scrubbed her stall every day, and he used boiling hot water and lye to do it. "Why?" asked Gertrude, when she went into the barn one morning and found him busy with his brush and his bucket. "We never scrub Maude's stall."

"When Sissy have her foal, we got to have a nice place for her, happen it comes at night or when it be rainin'."

But when Sissy's time came it was not night, and it was not raining. Allie had been to Grandma's to help her turn out her closets and air her winter things before they were packed away. She was coming back down the lane when she saw that Sissy was not grazing and was not even standing in her day-dreaming way. Instead she was lying down, then getting up, then lying down again, and she was sweating.

"Joe!" Allie ran to the barn. "Quick. I think Sissy's having her foal."

"Miss Allie, you go get your daddy."

Allie ran and found Papa at the dining room table with the books from the sawmill spread out in front of him. "Joe wants you," said Allie. "Something's happening with Sissy."

Papa grinned and went out, leaving the ink bottle open.

Mother put her sewing aside and closed the ink bottle. She went to the kitchen, where a stack of folded towels waited on the bench next to the water buckets. She unfolded them one after another and hung them on the line above the stove. "They'll be warm when the time comes to rub down the foal," she said.

She went out and Allie followed her. They saw the mare down in the grass. She was on her side with all four legs out. Papa knelt beside her and stroked her neck. Joe crouched and murmured softly to her, and suddenly the foal's hoofs appeared under her tail.

Mother stood at the fence and did not go nearer. Neither did Allie. Allie knew something about birthing, and the way small animals came slippery and wet from their mothers. Usually she was not frightened by it, but this seemed different. The mare was so big, and her baby had been so eagerly awaited.

Gertrude came running from down the lane, where she had probably been climbing trees. Then Tom Anderson appeared, and suddenly Allie felt awkward. It was all right for Papa and Joe to attend this birth, but not Tom. Tom had no business here. Or did Allie feel that way because Tom was her friend, and because human babies came the same way animal babies did, but with humans it wasn't to be spoken of between the sexes?

Papa turned around. For an instant Allie thought he might tell her to take herself away, and to take Tom with her. He didn't. He hardly seemed to see them. The foal was coming. The head appeared, brown and wet, and Sissy gasped and surged. Then the foal was out, its legs doubled under it and its head down as if it slept.

"Run and get the towels," Mother commanded.

Allie ran and was back in seconds. Joe took a towel and rubbed the foal, and still the foal seemed to sleep.

But soon Sissy was up. She licked and nuzzled her baby.

"Ain't she pretty?" said Joe to the mare. "You done good. Ain't you proud?"

The foal got itself up on its wobbly little sticks of legs. It was fuzzy-coated and beginning to dry, and Allie could see the white mark on its forehead. Joe coaxed it gently to the mare to begin taking her milk.

"She's going to nurse already?" said Tom. "I didn't think they did that so soon."

Allie turned away, feeling again that Tom should not be there. But he was not the least abashed. He watched and never left off watching, until Grandma came down the lane. Then he stepped aside to give her his place at the fence.

"It's a beautiful little horse," said Mother. She had not uttered a word the whole time, and she sounded now as pleased as if the whole idea of buying and breeding Sissy had been hers from the start.

"John picked the dam and John picked the sire," said Grandma. "Proud he should be, and I doubt not there will be more horses before long."

Tom beckoned Allie to follow him. She left the fence and walked a few steps up the lane. Tom said, "Tell your father I'll come later to see him. He won't want to be bothered now."

"To see Papa! What about?"

"About the job. My mother and father talked it over and they say I can go with him to the island."

Allie stood still and stared. She felt something almost like fright rising in her. Tom was going to the island? Why would Papa take Tom?

"What's the matter? Didn't you know? Your father wants me to start learning about his business so I can help him. With the fishermen. You know, with all that has to be done on the island."

Now Allie knew what the feeling was. It was envy that gripped her, and it was so strong that it was like a pain. "You're going with Papa?" Her voice was rough with anger. "But . . . but you can't even swim!"

She knew she couldn't swim either. She knew she sounded like Mother. She couldn't help it.

Tom stepped back away from her. "Well, yes. But your father will teach me to swim and . . . and I can help with the rowing. I can patch and clean up and all, and maybe some weeks I can help collect the rents. I don't know exactly what I'll be doing, but I want to try. If I do well, perhaps one day I can manage it all by myself."

Allie started away, forgetting the foal, forgetting Mother and Grandma there at the fence. She went a few feet up toward Grandma's house, then stopped. She saw the sheep grazing in the high meadow beyond the end of the lane. They were like big gray rocks except when they moved. And then Allie could not see them. Her eyes were wet and blurry.

"Allie, what's the matter?" Tom had come after her.

"It should be me!" she cried. "I should be going!"

But when she looked at him, he was miserable and anxious, and she softened. "It's all right," she said. "I know I can't go when all the fishermen are there. It . . . it wouldn't be proper. It's all right."

"Well," he said, "well . . . fine, then. I'll come back later."

He went off and Allie went back to the fence and watched the foal and tried to be as glad as she had been before. She almost managed it, and if the day was not quite what it had been for her, there was no one who noticed, and that was just as well.

Eight

"Allie, look!" Mother was at the window, her sewing in her hand.

Allie put the iron back on the stove to get hot. She went to the window and saw Uncle Hugh dashing past the house in his buggy. He never glanced around. And little wonder, thought Allie; Miss Jane Cameron was beside him, and he could not seem to look anywhere but at Miss Jane.

The buggy rattled on up to Grandma's gate. Uncle Hugh jumped down and turned with his arms out. Miss Jane leaned to him and let him lift her to the ground. He hugged her right there in broad daylight in front of Grandma's door.

"Oh!" said Allie, feeling an unaccustomed lurch in her stomach. It was not unlike the feeling she had had when the ocean swells dropped out from under Papa's boat on the way to the island.

"My stars!" said Mother. "Who is that with him?"

"It's Miss Jane Cameron," said Allie.

Uncle Hugh kissed Miss Jane then, and Allie said, "They're married!" The instant the words came out, Allie knew it must be so. There could be no other explanation for the two of them there together, kissing at Grandma's gate.

"My stars!" said Mother again. Then she ran out, not even waiting to take off her apron.

Allie went more slowly. She saw Grandma come out of her house, and she saw Uncle Hugh turn from hugging Miss Jane and begin to hug Grandma. Then Papa came across the meadow. He had been at Anderson's to give Tom a swimming lesson in the Anderson's pond. His hair was wet and his shirt stuck to this shoulders as if he had put it on while he was still soaked. He saw Uncle Hugh and Miss Jane, and he grinned and began to run.

Allie came up the lane at last. She heard Uncle Hugh say, "Mother, this is Jane. We were married yesterday."

"Aye," said Grandma. She looked at Jane and then at Hugh, and she nodded. "I've waited for this day."

Suddenly everyone was talking at once. Papa was shaking Uncle Hugh's hand and Mother was kissing Jane. Allie stood silent and watched. In a minute or two everyone went into the house. No one had even glanced at Allie, and she felt like a great gawk standing there in the lane.

Finally she went inside, feeling timid in this scene of grown-up jubilation. Uncle Hugh saw her and called to her to come and welcome her new aunt. The word "aunt" was strange. It made Jane suddenly seem older. When Allie went to kiss her, Jane glowed, and Allie thought of the lights in the church in Canso burning inside colored glass holders.

There was no cake in the house, so Grandma opened a tin of biscuits. Papa went to the cellar for sherry. As he poured it, Gertrude came racing in from the sawmill, where she had been watching Mr. Kelly as he went about his work. "Isn't that Uncle Hugh's buggy?" she cried. She saw Uncle Hugh and Jane, and stopped still and stared.

"Gertrude, come and meet your new aunt," said Uncle Hugh. He seemed to love saying that. Aunt Jane reached out. Gertrude stared for a second longer, then went to give Jane a shy, wondering kiss on the cheek.

Then they all heard Uncle Matt's tired old horse plod up the lane with the creaking old buggy behind it.

"I stopped at Matt's on the way," explained Uncle Hugh.

Grandma nodded. "Aye, 'tis them. I wonder it took Nonie this long to get here. She must have stopped to change her dress."

"Then she'll be the only one," said Mother, who had taken off her apron and put it in the kitchen.

Aunt Nonie came in with her eyes darting about in that searching way she had. Papa tried to pour a glass of wine for her, but she announced that it was far too early in the day for wine. Uncle Matt took a glass and Nonie scowled.

"Now you must tell us when you decided," said Grandma to Jane. "And where was the wedding? And what did your uncle and aunt have to say about it?"

Of a sudden the sparkle went out of Jane. "My uncle

83

and aunt were ... were ..." She looked helplessly at Uncle Hugh.

"They weren't at the wedding?" It was a gentle prompting from Grandma. Jane nodded.

Grandma's look changed suddenly. "And where was it you were married?"

Allie held her breath. If it was a magistrate who had presided over Uncle Hugh's vows, or a Protestant minister, there would be terrible trouble in Grandma's parlor.

But Uncle Hugh was smiling. "We were married in Halifax, Mother. A priest named Father Maginnis married us."

"Ah, well then," said Grandma.

Aunt Nonie's keen little eyes became keener still. She looked around the room as if waiting for someone to say something. When no one did, she spoke up. "Wasn't it a rather sudden decision?"

Allie saw her mother's lips tighten. It was the same question people had asked about the oldest Hurley girl. She had married Henry Bruce so suddenly, and the baby had been born scarcely seven months later.

Uncle Matt got a second glass of wine for himself and drank it down in one gulp. Allie saw his face, lean and white and miserable, like some wretched imitation of Papa's good looks. Her heart ached for him.

"Aye, the wedding was sudden indeed," said Uncle Hugh. "Three minutes after I laid eyes on Jane I decided I had to marry her. She's a deliberate piece, however, and it took her a month to decide she'd have me. Once she decided, Mrs. Cameron had to be told, and then there was such a talkation and a writing of lists as you've never seen."

"My aunt wanted me to have a big wedding," said Jane. "She wanted to order a Paris gown and have hothouse flowers, and I was to have enough clothes so that Hugh wouldn't have to get me anything for a year or more. We were to have a trip afterward, to go to England, perhaps, or Switzerland. It was going to be so much work!"

"And take such time!" cried Uncle Hugh. "A whole year, or perhaps longer, when Jane would be in Dartmouth and we wouldn't be together. It was too long to wait when we have only our lifetimes. So Jane wrote Mrs. Cameron a note and packed a valise, and we went to Halifax. We took the priest away from his supper. At first he said it couldn't be done right away. He said we would have to have the banns read in the church for three Sundays in a row. Well, if we had to wait for three weeks while he asked all the people in the parish if they had any objections to our marriage, Jane would have had to go back to the Camerons again, and Mrs. Cameron might have prevailed and made her wait for the big wedding, and we didn't want that.

"Finally the priest had us go out and bring in some of the people who were passing by the church. Then he stood up and announced three times that Hugh Hughes and Jane Cameron intended to marry. That took care of the banns. The housekeeper at the rectory was a witness, and the old man who looks after the churchyard was another. And we were married then and there."

"I didn't go back to the Camerons after that," said Aunt

Jane. "I thought I'd wait until my aunt had time to get used to the idea. I didn't want to hurt her. She's been good to me, and I *am* grateful!"

"I'm sure we're all grateful every day of our lives," said Grandma. "Gratitude is a becoming thing, since we get very little by ourselves. The good Lord must help us. Just the same, we can't be so grateful that we get mired in our tracks."

Grandma went to Jane and kissed her, and her old face was as soft and loving as ever it could be. Allie looked at Aunt Nonie. Nonie was watching Grandma and her face was like a stone.

Grandma beckoned to Allie and Gertrude to come help her. She started for the kitchen to get something that would serve for a wedding lunch.

On the way out Allie looked at Mother. She saw that Mother was not watching Grandma or Aunt Jane, but was looking at Papa. There was nothing stony about Mother. She looked suddenly as young and as glowing as Jane. Papa was holding her hand and stroking it, smiling to himself as if perhaps he was remembering the day he and Mother were married.

Aunt Jane and Uncle Hugh stayed on with Grandma for two days. In that two days everything on the Hughes farm seemed to sparkle. Mother sang and Papa whistled, and they laughed together as if they were living through their own courtship again. Gertrude was fascinated with her new aunt and followed Jane everywhere she went. Grandma looked suddenly younger, with roses blooming

86

pink in her wrinkled cheeks. Even Joe caught the joyful contagion. He sang softly as he went about his work.

The day after Uncle Hugh and Aunt Jane came, Allie awoke to the sound of her mother laughing in the kitchen below. She saw the splash of sunlight on the floor under the window, and she wondered why she had felt so glum the day before. She turned her head to look at Gertrude.

Gertrude was looking up dreamily at the ceiling. "When I grow up, I'm going to run off and get married, just like Aunt Jane. Everyone will be so surprised."

"I thought you were going to be a pirate when you grow up," said Allie.

"I'll marry a pirate," Gertrude announced. Then she bounced out of bed and began getting into her clothes.

Allie laughed and got up, glad of the sunlight and of Mother singing downstairs. And afterward she was to think of that day, and of the days and weeks that followed, as a time when it was warm and the sun always shone. Even after Aunt Jane and Uncle Hugh went back to Canso, it was a happy time, with Mother's mood continuing good, and with Papa keeping close to home except on the days when he and Tom went to Canso to see to the island.

After the first week or two, Allie did not mind greatly that Tom was going with Papa. Papa wanted someone who could really help with his business, and if that could not be Allie herself, it might as well be Tom. Besides, it was rather pleasant to go down early on Saturday morning and help Mother get the breakfast. Tom would come and sit sleepy-eyed in the corner and would sip his coffee and watch. He never said much. It was too early for talk. Just the same, it was comfortable to have him there.

It was a Saturday morning late in July when Uncle Matt came unbidden and unexpected. Papa and Tom had gone off hours before, and Mother and Allie were canning vegetables when Matt appeared. He had a new buggy, and there was a handsome bay mare hitched to it.

"My word!" said Mother. She went out to the gate. "Matt, that's an elegant rig!"

"The old mare died," said Uncle Matt. "I'm not sorry. She was a good enough horse in her day, but her day's been long past. This was Danny MacPherson's horse, and his carriage too. He was going to sell the horse in Antigonish, but I persuaded him to strike a bargain closer to home."

Matt sat with the reins in his hands and his eyes wandering out across the fields. "Where's Gertrude?" he asked.

There was something in his tone that must have frightened Mother. She took a step back, and her hands went to her throat. "She's . . . well, I don't know exactly. She took a book a while ago and went off that way." Mother pointed across the fields.

"George Chisholm came in this morning to get bullets for his gun," said Uncle Matt. "Three of his sheep were pulled down in the pasture last night, and two of John Kelleher's were killed on Thursday. He said it was dogs did it—that there's a pack of wild dogs roaming the countryside."

Joe came from the barn to take the horse. "Don't unhitch

her, Joe," said Uncle Matt. "I have to go on up the valley. But right now I have to find Gertrude. Then I'll talk to my mother. Nell, you and Allie go into the house and stay there. I'll be right back."

With that Uncle Matt set out across the meadow.

Nine

Allie and her mother were still in the lane when Grandma came out of her house and started down toward them. Shep roused himself from his nap in Grandma's dooryard and came too. The morning was hot, but Grandma had her shawl about her. She was often cold these days.

She stopped for a moment to look at Uncle Matt's new mare. "What brings Matt here?" she said, when she was close enough to speak. "I saw him go off across the meadow."

"He's gone to get Gertrude," Mother answered. "He says there are wild dogs loose in the neighborhood."

"Dogs?" Grandma pulled her shawl closer.

Mother told her what Uncle Matt had said about the sheep being killed. Then Mother and Grandma went into the house, and Grandma sat down in the kitchen rocker.

Allie hovered in the doorway. Shep had followed Grandma

90

as far as the yard and then had flopped down and put his nose on his paws. He looked as peaceful as could be.

"Mr. Chisholm must be mistaken," said Allie. "Dogs don't kill sheep."

"It could be wild dogs," said Grandma. "When I was a bairn, I remember a pack of dogs that came ravaging the countryside. My mother said it was the full moon drove them to do it. I think she was wrong. If the moon could make animals behave so, we would be fending them off so often we'd have time for little else."

Mother had busied herself putting the kettle on the stove. She shook her head now. "Mother, that sounds like one of those goblin stories they tell children to keep them quiet. I'll bet there were no dogs when you were little. I'll bet it isn't dogs now. It could have been wolves, though."

Allie did not relish the idea of wolves, but she was relieved to hear Mother say that. There was something unnatural about the idea of dogs killing sheep.

Uncle Matt was back before the kettle boiled. Gertrude was with him, and he had told her about Chisholm's sheep. Her eyes were wide with astonishment.

"Joe had better not turn the mares out to pasture today," said Matt. "I'll go talk to him. Mother, where are the sheep?"

"John moved them a week ago," said Grandma. "They're in the far pasture, yonder, at the edge of the woods."

"I'll send Joe to watch them. I brought a gun. And you'd better keep Shep in the house with you."

There was an urgency in his voice that told Allie he was afraid for them. He stood in the kitchen looking taller

91

than he usually did, and broader in the shoulders. It was as if he had grown somehow, just knowing that he could keep them all safe.

"Why do we have to stay in?" said Gertrude. "Do the dogs eat people too?"

"Let's hope not," said Uncle Matt.

"Matt, are you sure about this?" said Mother. "Dogs don't kill sheep. They just don't!"

Uncle Matt looked stern. "George Chisholm was very sure. And does it make a difference, Nell, whether it was dogs or something else? Would you be more comfortable with a pack of wolves in the neighborhood?"

"Well, no. Of course not."

"So stay safe inside until this is over. I'll go and talk to Joe, and then I'll warn the Andersons and the Shaws and the Munros. I'll be back before long."

He brought Shep in and then went across to the barn. Mother started to lock the door after him, but she must have realized that even the most determined dog—or wolf—could not turn a knob, for she let the door alone. She closed the windows, however. "I wish John were here," she said.

"Matt will see to everything," said Grandma. "Dinna be worryin' yerself."

Soon the buggy went past the house. Allie looked out and saw Joe come from the barn with a gun in the crook of his arm. He went off toward the far meadow.

Uncle Matt was gone until almost one. When he came into the house, he went to the sink to wash his hands.

"Was there trouble anywhere near here?" asked Mother.

"No, but that doesn't mean we're safe. Remember, George Chisholm's place isn't five miles away." He frowned. "It may not be wild dogs. The dogs might be mad."

"You mean they have hydrophobia?" said Allie. She had heard a terrible tale in the schoolyard about this disease. Timothy Hearne had a cousin in Truro whose dog had been bitten by a squirrel. The dog had developed hydrophobia, and Timothy's cousin had shot him. There was no help for it except to shoot him, Timothy had said. Nobody could cure hydrophobia.

"If it's hydrophobia," said Uncle Matt, "the dogs will get paralyzed before the end. Then they'll die, and the carrion crows will have to show us where to look for the bodies."

"People go mad," Gertrude pointed out. "Do they get hydrophobia and get paralyzed?"

"Gertrude, please!" cried Mother.

"People do go mad!" insisted Gertrude. "Old Mr. Kenner went mad. You said yourself he was mad as a hatter the day he yelled out in church that the Angel Gabriel was standing next to Father Murphy. But Mr. Kenner didn't hurt anybody. He just cried when his daughter took him away home."

"That was a different thing entirely," explained Grandma. "Sam Kenner is very old. Sometimes old people see things that are not really there. With the dogs it's a disease that they get when another creature bites them."

"It's called rabies," said Uncle Matt. "Rabies or hydro-phobia. The animal that gets it grows savage and will

93

attack anything that moves. But at the end the sickness paralyzes the animal, and it dies."

Allie looked at Shep. He lay close to Grandma, and he was dozing. She was glad he was neither savage nor paralyzed.

"If the dogs that killed the sheep aren't mad," said Uncle Matt, "they could be strays that have formed a pack. I've heard that strays in a pack can get very bold, and if they start pulling down livestock they keep on. They never go back to hunting small animals."

Allie shivered. A pack of hungry dogs might be even more dangerous than dogs with rabies. Hungry dogs would not get paralyzed and fall dead. They would keep running and killing.

Allie had set the table earlier. Now Mother put out cold meat, bread and butter, cheese, and some beans that were left from last night's dinner. They all ate, and when they were done Uncle Matt said, "Joe will watch the sheep through today, and I'll stay on in the meadow tonight. Nell, if you'll fix something for Joe, I'll take it to him. Then I think I'll go upstairs and stretch out for a while."

Mother went to the cupboard to get a plate for Joe's lunch, and Allie and Gertrude began to clear the table. Shep roused himself from his nap. He sat up and yawned.

"I'll take him out for a few minutes before I take Joe his lunch," said Uncle Matt.

Shep yawned again, then came slowly to Uncle Matt. He put his head on Matt's knee, and Matt scratched behind his ears.

"It's all pretty strange, isn't it, Shep?" said Matt. "Here

we've got to keep you indoors this beautiful day, when you should be out chasing squirrels like any sensible dog. And all because of a pack of outlaw animals that you wouldn't have a thing to do with."

The dog's tail thumped the floor.

Grandma stood beside the table, and Allie turned from the sink and saw her there. She was watching Uncle Matt. Matt went on talking softly to Shep. Then, almost idly, he put his thumbs on either side of the dog's muzzle and pushed up. The flesh lifted away from the teeth.

Allie saw a look of fright come suddenly to Grandma's face.

Uncle Matt leaned toward Shep. He was tense now, and the dog was trying to pull away from him. But he held Shep and he probed with his fingers at the dog's teeth. When he let go at last his fingers held something, and he sighed.

"It's wool," he said. "He's had wool caught in his teeth."

Grandma made a whimpering sound, and Uncle Matt went to her and led her to a chair. He made her sit, and the dog circled around until he was behind the chair. He stayed there, crouched flat, watching Matt.

"Ah, Shep, how could ye do so?" said Grandma.

"What . . . what is it?" cried Allie. "Uncle Matt, he couldn't have killed sheep! Not Shep! It couldn't be him!"

"Keep him in for now," said Uncle Matt. "I'll go to Chisholms and to . . . to Kelleher's. And some of the other neighbors. It's . . . We'll see. Keep him in."

He went out, forgetting that Joe was hungry in the

pasture. In minutes he had the horse hitched to the buggy and was off down the lane.

"Grandma?" Gertrude crept close to the old lady, and her voice was small and tearful. "Shep didn't eat Mr. Chisholm's sheep, did he? Not really? He couldn't."

"He does not bide in the house at night," said Grandma. "He never has, except it be bitter cold."

"But he helps to look after the sheep," said Gertrude. "When Papa moves them to a new pasture, he makes them go."

Grandma closed her eyes. "We maun wait and see."

They waited through the afternoon, with Shep huddled close to Grandma's skirt. The dog seemed to know that he was under suspicion. He would not look at any of them, but only crouched on the floor with his head on his paws.

Uncle Matt came back late in the afternoon. He left the buggy at the barn door and hiked off to get Joe. Allie saw the two of them come back together, their faces solemn. Joe went into the barn with the gun, and Uncle Matt came to the house.

He looked weary. There were lines in his face that Allie had not noticed before. He took a chair from beside the table and sat down near Grandma's rocker. "There's no sign of sickness in any of the dogs," he said, "but five of them at least have been at the sheep. Five besides Shep, that is."

Grandma sat unmoving, staring straight ahead. " 'Tis like the thing that happened so long ago," she said, and her old voice was high and quavery. "There's a madness

96

that can seize on animals and pass from one to the other, and it has naught to do with infection. It's that that ye be saying, is it not, Matthew?"

Uncle Matt had to clear his throat. "Charles Munro shot his two dogs," he said. "He did it right away, while I was still standing there. The O'Connor's dog had part of a sheep shank in the kennel. John O'Connor found it there. They think—we all think some stray came in from God knows where. Our dogs ran with him and saw him kill, and . . . and it must have been like the madness that comes over men when they run in a mob. They do things no one of them would ever do alone. The wild dog may be gone by now. Probably he is. But our dogs are . . . are still here, and . . ."

"Aye!" said Grandma, not making him finish the thought.

"Matt, what are you going to do?" Mother's voice came out in a whisper.

"The others are destroying their dogs," said Matt. "It's happening now, all through the valley. Munro is going up toward Boylston to warn the farmers there to look to their dogs. George Forsythe said he'd go out to the farms on the Canso road."

It was not real. Allie could not believe she was hearing it. Gertrude began to cry. "Shep didn't hurt the sheep! Uncle Matt, you aren't going to kill Shep, are you?"

He said nothing, but sat with his eyes on his mother's face.

"I can keep him in," said Grandma. "He can bide with me all the time and never go out at night or . . . or . . ." She stopped.

"If you want to take that chance," said Uncle Matt. "I will never go against you, Mother. I never have. But they say that once a dog has killed sheep, it will kill again. If he were to get out, and other dogs were to run with him, it could start over."

"And he would be the cause," said Grandma. She clasped her hands as if she might be praying. "And t'would be no life for him, shut up. He has never been a house dog. Ye maun take him away, Matthew, outside, and . . . and do what ye maun do."

"You're going to kill him!" Gertrude flew to Shep and hugged him around the neck. "No! You won't! I won't let you!"

Allie thought that Shep must have understood, for he pressed close to Gertrude and he trembled.

"He's not mad!" Gertrude screamed. "Look at him! He's like he always is!"

"Gertrude, we aren't sure why it happened, but we know it did happen," said Uncle Matt. He was pleading, but she would not hear.

"Liar!" she cried.

"Uncle Matt, even if he did it once, how can we say he will do it again?" Allie did her own pleading more gently. She could see that Uncle Matt was suffering with it all.

"It will happen again, Allie. It does. Anyone will tell you who's kept sheep. Once it happens, it happens again."

"You care more about the dumb sheep than you do about Shep," Gertrude cried. "Grandma, don't let him shoot Shep. We'll keep him here with us if you don't want him. Don't let him take Shep!"

Grandma shook her head. There were tears on her cheeks. "I dinna dare. There's no help for it."

Gertrude left off her shouting and bent double with sobs. Shep crept away and tried to wedge himself into the corner between the woodbox and the wall.

"If Papa were here you wouldn't do this!" Gertrude cried.

Mother took her shoulders and coaxed her away up the stairs.

Matt patted his leg. "Shep! Here, Shep!"

The dog cowered and would not go to him.

"Poor beastie," said Grandma. "He knows."

"He has a guilty conscience," said Uncle Matt. He reached for the loose skin on the scruff of the dog's neck. The dog tried to pull back. Grandma could not bear to see that.

"Matt, don't!" She waved Matt aside. "I'll take him. It will be easier if I do."

"Grandma, don't!" pleaded Allie. "You can't!"

"I can." She went to the dog and put her hand on his back, and she was able to lead him out. Uncle Matt followed them, and Allie went to the window. She did not want to watch, but she was not able to keep from watching. She saw Grandma get as far as the gate and then stop. Matt picked up the dog and carried him, there being no help for it. He disappeared behind the barn just as Gertrude came racing downstairs, all fresh rage.

"He could have waited!" she screamed. "Why does he have to do it now? Why not wait until Shep's asleep? I hate Uncle Matt! I hate him! I hate him!"

She snatched the sugarbowl from the table and threw it on the floor. It shattered and sugar flew everywhere.

Mother came and slapped Gertrude. Gertrude let out a short, sharp scream, then stood with her head against the wall and cried and cried.

Mother went into the parlor and closed the door.

Allie stepped over the bits of the sugarbowl, her knees shaking with shock. She went out to Grandma, who stood leaning on the gatepost. The gun went off as she took the old lady's arm, and she felt Grandma shudder as if it was herself who was shot.

At first Allie only stood and held Grandma's arm. But soon Grandma let go of the gatepost. She let herself lean on Allie, and the two of them walked up the lane to the big house. Allie made some tea and Grandma drank it. While she did, Allie sat beside her on a low stool, resting her head on Grandma's knee. She had sat that way many times when she was a tiny girl. Now the tears slid down her face to her chin and fell onto Grandma's skirt.

"There now," said Grandma. She put her hand on Allie's head. "It will pass. Everything passes at last."

Allie looked up at the wrinkled face. Grandpa had brought Shep home from Guysborough before Allie had ever been born. It was not possible to imagine the farm without Shep. How could Grandma bear it?

But she would. Allie knew it. She had already born the loss of Grandpa, and no doubt much else. Perhaps that was what it meant to be grown. If so, it was a hard thing, and Allie did not look forward to it.

Ten

"Where did you get him?" said Allie. She had been reading in the Sunday quiet of the parlor, and had come out when she heard Uncle Matt's buggy. She stared at the dog that crouched on the floor next to Uncle Matt's feet.

"Don't be too critical," said Uncle Matt. "He's the best I could do. There's a great shortage of civilized dogs in Guysborough. This one's been shut in old man Gates' cellar, so we know he hasn't had a chance to turn outlaw."

Allie looked at the animal and heard Uncle Matt chuckle. The dog had a tail that was too short for the rest of him, ears that were too long, and a matted coat that was dirty yellow and streaked. There was a look of terrier about him, but somewhere in his background there might also have been a spaniel.

"He's not a bit like Shep." Allie was doubtful.

"Of course he's not. But your grandmother has to have

a dog to fuss over and scold. It will work out. He can't take Shep's place, of course, but in time he'll make a place of his own."

Allie got into the buggy beside Uncle Matt and he drove on to Grandma's gate. Grandma and Mother came out to meet him. When she saw the dog, Grandma frowned.

The dog cringed, for all the world as if he were examining his conscience and finding his past filled with sin.

"Like as not he has fleas," decided Grandma.

"Yes, Mother," said Uncle Matt.

"I trust ye did na' pay good money for him."

"No, Mother," said Uncle Matt.

"Ah, well," said Grandma. "The big washtub is hanging in the pantry, Allie. Fetch it out."

Allie brought the tub out to the dooryard. She carried water from the reservoir on the stove and brought a jar of the soft soap that Mother made herself. Then Uncle Matt put the dog into the tub and held him so that he couldn't run away. Allie knelt to bathe him.

The dog was struck dumb by this outrage. He did not bark or whimper, but as Allie splashed the water up over his sides, he gasped.

Allie laughed. "He's holding his breath! He's afraid he'll drown!"

"Poor beastie!" said Grandma. "From the look of him he's not seen much kindness. I could cut my hand on his ribs."

Mother got some old towels from the closet and helped rub the dog down after his bath. Then Grandma took him into the kitchen. She filled a bowl with bits of meat, and the dog ate. He stopped every few seconds to look around, and he trembled as if he feared he would be driven from the food any minute, but he ate every morsel. Grandma washed his bowl and filled it with water, and he drank. When he was satisfied, Grandma sat down and coaxed him to come to her. She began to brush him with Shep's old brush.

Before Grandma finished the brushing, Gertrude came in. When she saw Uncle Matt, she turned her head away and would not speak to him. But then she saw the dog and she came close to look.

"Handsome animal, isn't he?" remarked Uncle Matt.

The dog was now used to being the center of attention. He looked around at Gertrude and yawned, then curled up at Grandma's feet to go to sleep.

"He's . . . he's ugly," said Gertrude.

"He is," replied Uncle Matt. He said it so agreeably that Gertrude smiled in spite of herself, and Allie decided that Gertrude would not really hate Uncle Matt forever. Probably she would not hate him for the rest of the afternoon.

Mother filled the kettle. After it boiled she made tea, and Allie felt the strangeness and the fright of the past day begin to disappear. When the dog woke and scratched at the door to go out, Allie put a rope around his neck so that he couldn't run away back to Guysborough. She took him out. Gertrude came too, keeping her distance at first, but finally putting her hand on the dog's head to feel the yellow fur. It was soft. The dog was braver now, and he wriggled with pleasure.

"He's not Shep," said Gertrude, "but I guess he's all right."

When Papa and Tom came home that night, the dog barked a quick bark at them, as if to let them know that he was guardian of Grandma's property. And by Monday morning Grandma had named the dog. He was to be called Rags, since he was a shaggy creature and not used to much. "And he will bide in the house at night," said Grandma. "I will na' see another animal die because I let him run in the moonlight. With any good fortune Shep might ha' outlived me. If he was old, I'm older still, and 'tis near my time to be carried to the kirkyard."

"Nonsense, Mother," said Allie's mother.

" 'Tis not nonsense," said Grandma. She said no more, and Allie was surprised she had said that much. Grandma did not approve of people who wearied their children with talk of death. The Chisholms had a grandmother who told them often that they would be sorry when she was dead and gone.

"I doubt na' that they will," Grandma had said when she heard of it. "They'll be sorry she did na' take it into her head to die sooner. There she is fretting her life away when she should be thankful for young faces around her and young voices prattling near her."

After a day or two Rags needed no rope to keep him from wandering. He followed Grandma eagerly as she went about her house. When she came down the lane to visit Mother and Papa, he trailed at her heels as far as the field where Joe was working with Sissy's foal, leading the little horse by the bridle to get her used to obeying commands. He dashed at Joe when he first saw the black man, and he barked. But Grandma spoke sharply and called him back, and he came, meek and repentant.

By September the dog was sleek and bold, and he knew his place and the place of every other creature on the farm. There was nothing new about him. It was as if he had been there forever.

Yet there was something new for Allie, and it was a thing she did not understand. It was a feeling that she was on the edge of something. She woke in the mornings and listened, wondering if the something had come, yet afraid that it might.

"When I grow up," said Gertrude, "I'll run off to sea. I'll marry a pirate and we'll live on a desert island. I'll sit up as late as I please, and no one will ever send me to bed."

Allie said nothing. She was nearer to growing up than her sister, and that frightened her.

She was in one of her wondering moods the day Joe put the lead rein on Sissy's foal and set the horse to trotting around and around him. Allie loved to watch Joe with the foal, which had been named Nell's Pride. Not that anyone ever called her that. Joe always spoke of her as Baby, and that was the name everyone used.

Allie leaned on the fence and listened to him talk to Baby and hold the rein and turn and turn and turn again, always facing the foal. When he clucked at her, Baby trotted faster, and when he tugged gently at the rein she slowed.

Allie saw Tom come around the corner of the barn. She

saw him suddenly as if she had not seen him for a long time. He was bigger than she remembered, and his shoulders were broader.

He came toward her smiling and said, "She's a great little horse, isn't she?" His voice was deep, the way a man's voice might be, and she saw that the buttons on his shirt pulled against the cloth. Soon the shirt would split at the seams, or the buttons would tear away.

Tom was brown from the sun, so that the freckles across the bridge of his nose did not seem to stand out so. He put his hands in his pockets, and she knew that the hands were calloused from pulling on the oars when he and Papa went to the island. He could swim now. She had not seen this, but she had heard Papa talk of it. He could keep his head above water if he had to, and Papa was relieved. That was just one more way that things had changed.

"Mr. Blanchard came back yesterday," said Tom now.

Allie sighed. Mr. Blanchard, the schoolmaster, boarded with the Andersons. Each spring he packed his belongings and made threatening remarks about leaving the valley for good. Then he went to his parents' home in Maine to help with the plowing and the planting. He always returned in the autumn browner and thinner than when he left, and with the threats of springtime forgotten.

"I'm not going back to school," said Tom. "I'm going to work with your father instead."

"I know," said Allie. She had heard her parents talk of it at the dinner table. Papa was pleased with Tom, so Tom could go on working for him, and one day Tom might manage the whole fishing business for Papa. But Allie would bide at home, and even though she had learned all that Mr. Blanchard could teach her, she would go to school. There had been talk of sending her to an academy in Halifax, but Mother and Papa thought she was not old enough to be so far from home.

"Mr. Blanchard will make me write a composition on what I did during the summer," said Allie. "He always does."

"What can you write?" said Tom. "One summer is like another. Things are always the same."

"No." Allie shook her head. "This summer was different. Sissy had Baby. There were the dogs that ran wild. Grandma has Rags now, instead of Shep, and . . . and everything is different."

She looked eagerly at Tom. She wanted him to say, "Oh yes! You noticed that, did you? It *is* different now."

He did not say it. He was not even looking at her. He had a splinter in his thumb, and he was trying to work it out with the tip of his pocket knife. "Um-hm!" he said, as if he hadn't been listening—or as if he didn't care what she was telling him.

She wanted to shout. She wanted to double her fists and box his ears.

"You're going with Papa tomorrow," she said instead. She knew it sounded like an accusation.

"Sure. We go every week, don't we?"

Allie gritted her teeth. All the things that had happened— the way Gertrude had screamed when Uncle Matt shot Shep, the way Grandma had stood holding to the gatepost when the gun went off—Tom had not seen those things.

If he had seen, would he have cared? And he was happy enough to see her when she was near, but did he mind when she was not there? Not really. He would go to Canso with Papa tomorrow, and he would not think of her on the way. Perhaps Papa would not, either. She felt a stab of grief. She hated Tom.

She turned and started away.

"Allie, wait!" Tom called after her.

She did not hesitate. She marched down the lane and into the house.

Mother was in the kitchen, but Allie did not look at her or speak to her. She went up the stairs to the room she shared with Gertrude, and she hated Mother, just as she hated Tom.

"Allie?" Mother came up the stairs.

Allie turned away. She had a lump in her throat and she did not want to talk.

"Allie, what is it? Don't you feel well?"

Allie looked out the window at the sunlit fields. "I'm all right," she said.

"I heard Tom call you. Did you quarrel with him?"

Allie shook her head.

Mother waited a moment longer, then went back downstairs. Allie sat on the bed. She was sorry she had run away from Tom. He didn't know he had done anything wrong, and she didn't know how to tell him. She decided not to go out again. He would forget that she had run off, the way he forgot about the dogs. The way he forgot everything.

At that the tears came. The sunlight was thin already.

In the evenings the breeze from the sea was cold. Autumn was upon them, and before too long winter would come. And what of it? her mother would say if Allie were to speak of it. Or perhaps she wouldn't say that. It was hard to tell about Mother.

The tears passed. Mother called from the foot of the stairs for Allie to come and set the table. Allie went down and began to unfold the cloth. Mother did not ask questions, but Allie felt her watching, and resentment pricked at her. It was not fair! Why should Allie spend time sensing Mother's moods, testing the air to see if Mother was pleased or cross? She wanted to say, "Don't watch me! Leave me alone so I can go upstairs and cry. It's what I want to do, and I don't care what you think about it!"

"You don't really have to go to school this year," said Mother suddenly. "You could stay at home and help me. But your father is afraid you'll get out of the habit of studying if you stay home. Perhaps that's not right. Or perhaps you *are* old enough to go to Halifax . . ."

"No!" said Allie quickly.

Mother stared. "I thought you wanted to go."

"I do. I do, Mother. I'm sorry. I only mean . . . I don't want to go right now. It's too soon!"

Allie cried again, and Mother did not shush her or tell her not to be silly. She let her cry, sitting hunched on one of the straight chairs.

Gertrude came in. "What's the matter?" she asked.

"Nothing, Gertrude. You can finish setting the table.

Allie doesn't feel well. She'll have her supper upstairs on a tray."

Which was what happened. Allie went upstairs and Gertrude brought her a tray. She ate sitting by the window and watching the fields grow dark, and she did not answer any of Gertrude's questions.

Eleven

Papa and Tom were off in the morning almost before the first light. Allie heard Joe bring the buggy from the barn, and she wanted to get out of bed and go down, but she did not. She had been so strange last night. She had not seen Papa at all, and she had run away from Tom. How could she explain this?

But perhaps they would not even wonder. She would wait, she thought. Tomorrow night, by the time they returned from Canso, they would have forgotten and things would be easy among them again.

Gertrude scrambled into her clothes and went downstairs with her face unwashed and her hair uncombed. Allie lay listening to the voices in the kitchen. Tom was there. She could picture him sitting sleepily in the corner, out of the way while Papa had his breakfast.

Then the door opened and Papa's step was quick in the dooryard. The buggy springs creaked.

Allie got up then. She went to the window and saw Papa and Tom drive down the lane. Once Papa looked back and waved, and Allie knew it was Mother he waved to.

She dressed and went down. Gertrude was at the table eating oatmeal. Mother said nothing except, "Are you hungry? You didn't have much supper last night." She did not wait for Allie to answer, but spooned out a bowl of oatmeal for her.

Allie ate the oatmeal, and some bread and milk besides, and the day went on as summer Saturdays usually did. Allie helped Mother change the sheets on the beds, and she pulled some weeds from the kitchen garden. Gertrude helped until she grew bored with weeds, and then she wandered off alone. Joe went back and forth between the barn and the pasture where the new mares grazed, and for a while he worked with Baby. And through the whole day there was the drone of the sawmill starting, rising to a high whine, then breaking off.

Late in the afternoon there was a sudden change in the light. The sun was gone, and the wind gusted at the trees. Allie was picking some beans for supper when Mother called, "See where Gertrude is. I think it's going to rain." Almost before she finished speaking the drops were spattering down.

Allie carried her potful of beans inside, took a shawl, and set out down the lane. Uncle Matt was coming up in his new rig, with Gertrude beside him. He had come upon her perched in one of the apple trees along the lane, blissfully ignoring the rain and trying to decide whether any of the apples were ripe enough to eat.

She jumped down when the buggy reached the gate, and stood with her hand on the gatepost, looking at the sky and at the rain coming down. It was more than a spattering of wetness now. It was a downpour, and the wind was loud in the trees. Uncle Matt went on toward the barn.

"Come in!" cried Allie. "You'll get soaked!"

"It's really stormy isn't it?" said Gertrude. "Do you think it's storming in Canso too?"

"I suppose so," said Allie. She knew that it was early for one of the autumn storms to come, and yet the storm was here. She remembered Papa at the oars, and the sun turning the seas to green hills, and the boat coasting up the hills, then sliding down. But the water would not be glowing and green now. It would be gray.

She thought then of the miles between Guysborough and Canso, and then the miles of sea between Canso and the island. The buggy had gone off so early that morning; they must have reached Canso early in the afternoon. If they had gone to the island, they were safe there now. They would stay until the storm passed and the seas were calm.

Allie and Gertrude were wet through. "Go and change," said Mother. "Gertrude, don't throw your dress down in a lump on the floor. Hang it on the hook. Or better still, bring it down with you and I'll dry it over the stove."

Mother seemed concerned with cutting the beans and drying the clothes and getting supper on the table, and

Allie found that reassuring. While she and Gertrude changed, the wind slackened and did not roar so loudly. The squall was dying as quickly as it had come up.

Grandma and Uncle Matt came to supper that evening. Uncle Matt had driven out to bring some things that Grandma wanted from the store, and he was glad of the invitation to stay on. By the time they sat down at the table the storm had died completely. Allie felt that the house was warm and cozy and snug, and she wondered why she had been so angry and sad yesterday. She was glad that her spell of moodiness has passed.

The next day was the Sunday the priest came from Canso to say Mass in the church which the O'Connors had built on their property. This was an event that happened only one Sunday out of four. It was the occasion of much scrubbing and pressing and primping. Uncle Matt had spent the night at Grandma's, and he took Mother and Grandma in the buggy. Allie and Gertrude walked, and on this particular Sunday Joe came out of the barn, shining and brisk and smelling strongly of soap. He announced that he would like to come with them if they did not mind.

"Do you want to be a Catholic?" said Gertrude.

"I reckon not," said Joe, "but I ain't put my foot inside no church since I come here, and it doan do none of us no harm to pray."

Joe trailed behind Allie and Gertrude. He would not walk beside them because he felt that there might be some unpleasantness if he did. "Folks sometimes plainly thinks bad of it," he said, "like I be takin' liberties I ain't got no call to take." When they reached the church he did not sit with them, but stood in the back. Now and then Allie looked around to see him there.

The church was a plain little building, whitewashed inside, with windows that were pointed at the top and had frosted glass in them as a humble substitute for stained glass. The Mass was a low Mass, but there were two of the Chisholm boys to serve, the older one with a cassock so short that his trouser legs looked out from under it. Mrs. O'Connor had gathered bunches of wild flowers for the glass vases on the altar, and the candles sparked gleams of light on the chalice and sent ripples of brightness over the green silk of the priest's vestment. Allie knelt and listened to the patter of Latin between the priest and the boys who served him, and the feeling of warmth and belonging was strong in her.

When the Mass was over and they were on their way home, Joe said that he thought Mass was a beautiful way to pray except that nobody but the Lord could understand all those strange words.

"The Mass is in Latin," said Gertrude. "That's so it's the same everywhere."

"And Latin is a language that nobody uses, so it won't change," Allie pointed out.

"I suppose not," said Joe. "Wouldn't nobody know how to change it, would they?"

Allie laughed and decided that Joe had a way of going directly to the point.

Joe vanished into the barn when they got home. Soon Allie and Gertrude could hear the soft, formless music that he made with his harmonica. Gertrude wanted to go fishing, and at first Mother said that she couldn't, since she was dressed in her best dress.

"It will soon be too cold," argued Gertrude. "Let me go now. I'll change my dress."

Mother relented, and Gertrude ran upstairs shouting for Allie to come and unbutton her. Allie went up and was undoing Gertrude's buttons when Gertrude said, "Why don't you come too?"

Allie realized then that it had been a long time since she had gone to the brook with Gertrude. There always seemed to be something her mother wanted her to do in the house. She went to the top of the stairs, but she did not ask for permission to go. Instead she called, "I'm going with Gertrude."

"All right," said Mother. "Try to keep her fairly dry."

So Gertrude unbuttoned Allie, and Allie put on her oldest skirt, and the two went out to the barn to get the fishing lines. Gertrude's was ready, but Allie's was a tangle. It had not been used all summer. Joe stopped playing his harmonica and helped her untangle it, even though she did not really care whether she fished or not. She only wanted to be out under the wide sky. Then Joe dug a hole for them out behind the barn and helped them pick worms out of it before the poor blind things could burrow back out of sight.

Gertrude was enthusiastic about fishing, but most days she caught nothing, perhaps because she waded into the water as often as she did anything else. She picked up stones and wet the hem of her dress. Now and then she did catch a fish.

This was not one of the days. The stream that ran through the Hughes farm came down from the high land to the south. It meandered along on the far side of the pastures, just at the edge of a wood. The girls reached it that day to find it chilly in the shade under the oak trees. Allie did not even bait her hook. Instead she found a place where she could sit in the long grass and let the sun shine on her. She turned her back on the stream and listened with half an ear while Gertrude talked to her, and sometimes to herself, and frequently to the fish. "It's a delicious worm," she told the fish. "Joe caught it just for you. Try a taste! Come on!" But the fish were deaf or indifferent.

Allie looked back the way they had come. She saw her house and the barn, and she thought she could hear Joe's harmonica. She saw Grandma's house at the top of the lane. There were more fields and woods beyond the house. And far off, out of sight, she knew there was the sea. It would be blue today under a blue sky, just as blue as it was that day she and Papa had stood on the top of the island and looked out to the place where the sea curved up to meet the sky.

She watched sleepily as Grandma came out of her house. Rags was with her. Then Uncle Matt came out too. He gave his arm to Grandma, and he and Grandma and Rags walked down to Allie's house. Mother opened the door for them, and they went in.

Allie knew they would sit in the parlor now. They would drink tea and talk of the horses in the meadow. Perhaps

Uncle Matt would tell of the goings-on in Guysborough. Allie closed her eyes, feeling warm and content, as if she could stay forever in the grass with the wind gentle all around her.

The afternoon went by. Gertrude splashed about, and Allie saw Joe go up toward the meadow where the mares were kept. A while later there was a carriage in the lane. It was coming slowly. Allie stood, wondering who it might be. She saw it was Uncle Hugh's rig, and she was almost sure that Aunt Jane was sitting beside Uncle Hugh.

She felt a twinge of uneasiness. Why were Uncle Hugh and Aunt Jane here when Papa was in Canso, or perhaps somewhere on the road between Canso and Guysborough?

She looked around at Gertrude and saw that Gertrude was watching the carriage too. There was a shadow of a frown on her face.

The two of them did not speak, but Gertrude put down her line without bothering to wind it in. They set out across the meadow, watching the carriage every step of the way. By the time they were halfway to the lane they were running. Allie flew past the barn and was out in front of the rig when Hugh reined in his horse at the gate.

Joe came from the barn. He went to hold the horse's head, and he looked up at Uncle Hugh. Allie saw a watchful, wary look come to his face.

Uncle Hugh got down from the carriage and lifted Aunt Jane down. Jane looked at Allie and Allie saw that she had been crying, and she looked as if she might cry again.

Gertrude made a strangled sort of sound behind Allie. She took hold of Allie's arm, and her hands were cold.

"What?" said Allie. She was staring hard at Aunt Jane, and the question was only a hoarse whisper. "What is it?"

Mother appeared in the doorway, and Uncle Hugh and Aunt Jane went toward her, with Jane not answering Allie, but only shaking her head.

Allie and Gertrude left Joe in the lane. When they got as far as the hall they needed to go no further. Uncle Hugh had stopped there, and he stood with his head bowed so that he did not look at Mother. Grandma was in the parlor door.

Uncle Hugh cleared his throat. "John was . . . a little later going to the island yesterday than he usually is. It was . . . when the wind came up yesterday afternoon, he could have been on the open sea in that boat and . . . and still I didn't worry. He's an experienced hand. But this morning, just to be sure, I went down to the pier and I waited for a while and . . ."

He stopped and drew a deep breath. "When it was ten and he didn't come, I rowed over to the island myself, just to put my mind at ease."

His voice seemed to come from a great distance. Allie closed her eyes, but then the floor tilted under her, so she opened them quickly, afraid she would fall if she could not see the walls around her. She was dreaming. It was a terrible dream. She wanted to wake.

Uncle Hugh went on. "I talked to the fishermen at the island."

"John was not there?" said Mother. Her voice was rough. "You went and you did not find John, that's what you're saying?"

"He hadn't reached the island," said Uncle Hugh. "He left Canso before the gale, and the wind came up so suddenly."

"If he did not reach the island, he went ashore someplace else." Mother sounded angry. "He is someplace down the coast. Or on another island. Why do you come hurrying here? Why aren't you in Canso? Why aren't you making the men look for him?"

It was being hard for Uncle Hugh. He looked at Mother with such a pleading in his face, as if he said, "Please! Please! You must let me stop speaking about it."

Then he spoke aloud, going doggedly on. "The men put out in boats. The men who were on the island, you know. Nell, they found one of his oars. There is always a chance, I think. But they did find the oar. But they will keep on with the searching."

Allie could see those oars again, with Papa's initials carved on the shaft. She remembered Papa handing them to Mr. McIver, and McIver putting them in the little shed at the dock. Papa had been in that small boat—Papa and Tom—and the water had not glowed green with sunlight. There had been the wind, and the water would have been gray. Had it come in over the sides?

Papa could swim. Tom could swim, but only a little.

"You came too quick!" Mother said, sharp and shrill. "You should have waited. If he upset, he is with the boat. Why didn't you wait?"

Allie felt Gertrude press close to her, and she saw Mother's face stony with rage. Uncle Hugh shook his head, not able to say more. Aunt Jane moved as if she would touch Mother, but Mother raised a hand and Jane flinched as though Mother would strike her.

Grandma was still there in the doorway, and she looked tinier than ever. Uncle Matt's arms were around her to hold her up, for she was limp.

Suddenly Mother screamed a scream such as Allie had never heard. She whirled around and disappeared into the dining room.

"Mother!" Gertrude tried to get past Uncle Hugh to go to her, but Uncle Hugh caught her shoulder and began to draw her into the kitchen.

Then metal struck on something in the dining room, and struck and struck again. Again Mother screamed, and something crashed.

They pushed and bumped getting through the hall and into the dining room.

"Nell, your beautiful stove!" cried Aunt Jane.

Mother kept at it, beating at the porcelain stove with a poker, beating it and beating it to pieces. "What good is it?" she cried. "What good is it? What good is any of it?"

Twelve

In those first days Allie did not cry. The news that Uncle Hugh had brought did not seem real. It had not happened. It could not happen to Papa.

Gertrude cried. Sometimes at night she lay very quietly next to Allie, and Allie knew she was crying only by the shaking of the bed. And sometimes the weeping was wild and noisy, and Allie would stroke her arm. Gertrude would grow quieter then, and at last she would sleep.

Then Allie would lie in the darkness, and her mind would dart this way and that, trying to find a way for Papa to be alive, and Tom with him. She would see the ocean again, and would think how it must have been with the waves breaking over the sides of the boat. The boat had been swamped, or upset. And then?

Then Papa and Tom would have held fast to the boat. That was what one did when a boat upset. One stayed with the boat. The fishermen always said that a boat will not sink, even when it's overturned. So Papa and Tom had clung to the boat and drifted on the sea. And then they had come ashore on some lonely island. They were on that island now, waiting for a passing ship to find them and bring them home again. Or perhaps they had come ashore to the south, in Maine. So shocked and sore were they that Papa had lost his memory. So had Tom, and now they were trying to get home without knowing where their homes were. It could have happened.

Allie did not share these desperate hopes with Mother. She could not talk to Mother. These days Mother was like a wounded creature. Sometimes when she looked at Allie and Gertrude, she did not seem to see them.

On that terrible Sunday Aunt Jane had coaxed Mother to bed after she had worn her throat sore with screaming, and after the stove was completely in splinters. Grandma had sat huddled in the parlor until Mother was upstairs and quiet at last, and then Grandma had cried as Allie had never seen her cry—not even when Grandpa died. Uncle Hugh had sat with her, looking gray and exhausted, and when Uncle Matt had asked who would tell the Andersons, Hugh had made a motion with his hand and had shaken his head. He had told Mother and Grandma, and he could do no more. So Uncle Matt had gone carrying a lantern from the barn, for by that time it was dark. Allie did not know what Uncle Matt had said to Tom's mother and father, or how the Andersons had behaved. They did not come to the Hughes house, and Mother did not go to the Andersons'. Allie wanted to go, but she was afraid. If

123

Mrs. Anderson screamed out as Mother had, she would not know what to do. Besides, if she even spoke of Tom's death, it would mean that he truly was dead, and Papa with him. Allie was not ready to admit that.

After a week the dory washed ashore a few miles from Guysborough. The man who found it had heard about Papa and Tom, and he sent for Uncle Matt. When Allie learned about the dory she knew that Papa and Tom had not been able to stay with the boat, and the pain that was inside her grew worse. It was a pain like hunger, except that Allie could not ease it, no matter how often she went to the kitchen to eat bits of bread or leftover meat or potatoes.

After the boat was found there was a service for Tom Anderson at the Protestant church in Guysborough. Mother refused to go. Some of the time she declared that Papa was not dead. Some of the time she would not hear Papa spoken of at all. And some of the time she was bitter against Tom Anderson. Papa would be safe at home, she said, had Tom not been with him. Tom did not swim well, and Papa had died trying to save him. Mother did not plan to mourn the boy who had caused his death.

When Mother spoke so Allie wanted to scream, "Must you always be placing blame? Why do you have to hate Tom? Tom died too, remember?" But Allie did not say this, for she saw that her mother was in agony.

Allie and Gertrude went with Grandma to Tom's service. Allie cried at last. The minister talked of Tom as being in the very bloom of his youth, and full of promise, and Allie remembered him as he was on that last day, brown from the sun, with his shoulders too broad for his shirt. And she had run away from him, and had never said goodbye to him, and now he was dead. And having wept for Tom, she knew that truly Papa was gone, and she was racked by such a storm of sobbing that Aunt Nonie and Uncle Matt had to take her out to the church steps. Uncle Matt held her on his lap and Nonie crouched beside her. She knew they wanted to help, but they could not. No one could help.

The service ended and people came out in a stream. Grandma and Gertrude stopped on the porch. People spoke to Grandma, and she answered them quietly enough and put up her cheek so that Mrs. Anderson could kiss it. Mrs. Anderson bent to kiss Allie too. Then, when everyone was gone but the Hugheses, Allie recovered herself enough to think that the service had not been long, and everyone was quick enough to go off about their business. Somehow more should have been made of poor Tom.

It was almost a month before there was a Mass for Papa. Mother would not have it sooner, and she would not have any word of it said to the neighbors since she could not bear to hear anyone around her speak of Papa. Only Matt and Nonie and Jane and Hugh came to the little church in the Intervale. The Chisholm boys were there to serve, and Allie looked around once and saw that Joe had come to stand silent and alone at the back of the church.

Uncle Hugh had a stone with Papa's name and his dates put up in the churchyard near Grandpa's grave. Allie did not go near it until the day in November when she looked out and saw Grandma on the lane. The wind was blowing up the valley from the sea, but Grandma had on only a thin shawl. When she saw that Grandma did not intend to stop at the house, Allie took another shawl and went out to her.

"You must be cold," she said.

"And I'll soon be colder yet," Grandma replied.

It was a thought to make a bleak day more bleak still. Grandma took the shawl and held Allie's arm, and together they walked down to the road. Allie had guessed that it was to the churchyard Grandma was going, and when she saw the stone for the first time she felt no rage. Her bitter grief was tempered, but in its place there was a great loneliness, for she would not see Papa ever again.

" 'Tis a cruel thing to lose a child," said Grandma. "Your father should have lived many a day. He should have lived to see you well wed and with your own bairns about you. And Gertrude too." Grandma sighed. "The Lord giveth and the Lord taketh away. Blessed be the name of the Lord."

Allie was glad that Gertrude was not with them. Gertrude would not have blessed the Lord; she felt that He was not tending properly to His business these days.

Grandma turned from the new stone and looked at Allie. "You're tired, child," she said.

Allie wanted to say that she did not sleep well, but what good would it have done? Grandma would worry. "I'm all right," she said.

Allie and Grandma left the new stone, and Grandma went to stand for a few moments at the stone that marked

Grandpa's place. Then they went back to the road and walked under the trees that were dropping their leaves. There had been ice on the puddles that morning. Allie knew that soon winter would be upon them. She dreaded the long months when they would be shut in the house and the days would end with the darkness that came in the afternoon, and the evenings would be long and quiet without Papa to tell his stories and dream his dreams and plan his ventures. There would be only Joe in the barn with the horses to remind them that things had been so different before.

She and Grandma turned in at the lane and walked past the sawmill. The mill was quiet now. Mother had announced one day that she could no longer pay Mr. Kelly, and she had dismissed him. This had made no sense to Allie, and it had not made sense to Uncle Matt either. He had come from Guysborough to argue for keeping Mr. Kelly. He had tried to show that the sawmill always brought in money, and that it would continue to do so. Mother had refused to listen and had shut herself up in her room, crying that he did not understand—that no one understood. And Uncle Matt had gone back to Guysborough, saying only that it was a hard time for Mother, but that it would pass.

When Allie and Grandma reached the gate, Grandma decided that she would come in. They found Mother in the parlor, sitting at Papa's desk with one of Papa's account books open in front of her. She put down the pen with which she had been scribbling figures on a piece of paper. Grandma went to her and took her hand.

"Well, child?" said Grandma. "How is it today?"

Grandma spoke as if Mother were very young. Mother did not seem to notice. Or perhaps she did not care. "Good enough," she said. Then suddenly she said, "No. Not good enough. Mother, I can't stay here."

"Ah," said Grandma.

"Not in this house," said Mother. "I see John everywhere."

"Aye," said Grandma. "What will ye do then? Will ye go to Antigonish to your kin there?"

"No. There's no one left there but my aunt. No. I've had a letter from my sister Susan. I can go to Boston, to her."

Grandma nodded. "And how long will you bide with her? For the winter?"

Mother got up and went to look out of the window, perhaps so she would not look at Grandma. She seemed to have forgotten that Allie was there, and Allie watched, fascinated and afraid.

"I think I won't come back," Mother said.

"Not come back?" Grandma said that and then said nothing.

Allie stood silent near the door. Mother could not mean it, she thought. Perhaps it was just the long, lonely winter she could not face. In the spring she would feel differently.

"This is the girls' home," said Grandma at last. "They were born here, like all the Hugheses, and . . ."

"I know about all the Hugheses and I don't care!" cried Mother. "Allie's children won't be Hugheses, will they?

128

Or Gertrude's? They'll be something else, and there's an end to the Hugheses! There'll be no more!"

"There's not an end!" cried Grandma. "Even if Jane's babe . . ."

"What?" It was a shriek from Mother. "Jane is expecting?"

Grandma was still for an instant. Then she said, "I should na' have said it. We did na' wish to tell ye so soon. In April, as near as she can tell, she'll have her child."

"Oh, God!" cried Mother.

"Ellen!" Now Grandma's voice was sharp. "Do ye want the world to stop because ye've lost your man?"

"She'll probably have a son," said Mother.

"And if she does?"

"It's not fair!" cried Mother.

"Life isn't fair. And what is it to you and the girls? This is still their home. Hugh and Jane will na' come to put them out on the road!"

"How very kind of them!" There was a world of bitterness in Mother's voice.

"Ah, then," said Grandma, her voice soft again. "Go to your sister in Boston if ye must. Take the girls. But dinna be headstrong. Leave the way open for yourself so ye can come back if ye find it cold in Boston."

"And bring the girls back so they can play second fiddle to Jane's son?"

"The bairn is na' born yet," said Grandma. "Let's not speak ill of it. Allie and Gertrude are John's children, and they will play second fiddle to no one. Don't take them

129

away from their place. They've lost something too, but must it be so much?"

Mother did not answer this, so after waiting a brief time, Grandma went out. Allie went too, so that Grandma could hold her arm going up the lane. When they stopped at the gate, Grandma looked full into Allie's face. "Be careful of your mother, Mary Alice," she said. "And be careful of yourself too, and your sister. Your mother has a pain that blinds her."

The old lady went in, and Allie went home to the house where it seemed that time had frozen. As she passed the barn she heard Joe's harmonica, and she wondered if time had not frozen for Joe too. He went on training Sissy's foal and he tended to the mares. He had not been off the farm since Papa's funeral. It was as if he were waiting for something. Allie wondered if it might be for Mother to dismiss him, as she had Mr. Kelly. And then Allie wondered what they would do if Mother did send Joe away. Who would see to the horses? Or would the horses go too? And if they all went, what would happen to Grandma? Who would carry wood for her and bring in water?

Gertrude was in the kitchen spreading a piece of bread with jam. "Mother's in the parlor adding things up and talking about how poor we are," she said. "Are we really poor?"

"I don't know." Allie did not think they could actually be poor. There was the sawmill. It could make money if Mother would let Mr. Kelly run it. In the spring the mares would drop their foals. Before too long Sissy's Baby might

130

be sold. Joe could see to the horses, but Mother had to give the orders.

Allie thought of the island. No one had dared mention the island to Mother. It was a sore subject. Just the same, it was there, and it could be turned to account. But Mother did nothing but sit in the parlor and add and subtract figures and talk of poverty.

And now she talked of leaving everything and going away.

A week after the conversation with Grandma, Uncle Matt and Uncle Hugh came with a man named Jensen. This man spoke with a strange, different accent, and he wanted to buy Papa's sawmill.

Allie was not asked to join Mother and the uncles in the parlor, nor had she expected to be asked. But she felt that she had a right to know what was happening, so she sat on the stairs and listened through the open door.

Grandma had come for the meeting, and when she heard Jensen's offer for the sawmill, she lifted her hand for attention. Her sons turned to her.

"Dinna sell the land," she said.

"Oh, the land!" said Mother. "It's Hughes land, isn't it? I forgot that it mustn't be sold! And what am I to do? Walk away and leave the mill to stand idle?"

"You can sell the business without selling the land," said Uncle Hugh.

From her perch on the stairs Allie could not see her mother. She saw only the corner where Mr. Jensen sat like a pale and amiable statue.

"If you lease the sawmill to Mr. Jensen," said Uncle Hugh, "you'll have money coming in every three months."

"Every month," said Mother, her voice sharp.

There was silence in the parlor for a moment. Then Allie saw Jensen nod. There was talk about how much money he would send to Mother, and the matter was settled. Mr. Jensen would have the business and Mr. Kelly would help him as he had helped Papa. Like Papa, Mr. Jensen had other businesses. Mother would get her money every month, no matter how much lumber came from the mill, or how little.

With the matter of the sawmill settled, there was the question of the lease on the island. It still had nine years to run. A young man named Alec MacDougall came from Canso to talk of it. He wanted to take the lease over and to pay Mother a share of the profits he would make on the fishing business. It was not a big share, but it was young MacDougall who would have the work of the business. Allie's heart ached to think of a stranger having the say about Papa's island, but Mother wanted only to have done with it and never think of the island again. The papers were soon signed, and Grandma said, "You'll be well fixed in Boston."

But there were still the horses in the barn. A few days later, men began to come to look at the horses and to talk with Joe. Often they walked in the lane and talked with Uncle Matt or Uncle Hugh. Allie was watching from the kitchen the day a man with a red mustache came and spent a long time in the barn. He came out and Allie saw him shake hands with Uncle Matt. She guessed that he had made a good offer. Uncle Matt brought him into the house to see Mother. Mother sent Allie and Gertrude upstairs, and on the way Gertrude stayed close to Allie. She often did so these days.

"I hope she doesn't sell Maude," said Gertrude.

"She can't," said Allie. "Grandma will need Maude."

"What about Joe? What will Joe do after Mother sells the mares?"

"He'll have to leave," Allie predicted. "One of the neighbor boys will have to come and do for Grandma."

The kitchen door opened below. The girls looked out and saw Mother go up the lane with the visitor. Uncle Matt was with them, and Joe came from the barn to meet them. Joe's dark face was mournful.

The man left that day with Sissy and Baby tied to his buggy. The next day a different man came for the other horses. They all went but Maude. The day after that Joe left with his belongings done up in a bundle. Uncle Matt was to take him in the buggy, but before Matt arrived, Joe knocked on Grandma's door. Allie was there, and she let him in and watched him stand tall and thin in his threadbare clothes.

Grandma told him what a wonderful hand he had been with the horses, and he made a little bow that was scarcely more than a nod. "If'n ah kin take the liberty, Miz Hughes," he said, "ah will come askin' about you when ah'm in this paht of the country. It grieves me to think you be here all alone when you lost your own baby."

Allie had rarely thought of Papa as Grandma's baby, but of course he had been. Grandma had carried him in

133

her arms and nursed him and watched him grow. Now she had lost him, and now she would lose Allie and Gertrude too. They would go far away to an aunt who was hardly more than a name. And now Allie knew with a cutting sharpness that she might not see Grandma again, for it was true that Grandma was old.

Allie's eyes filled and she turned away so that no one would see. She heard Joe go out. The door closed on him, and it was one more ending.

Mother wanted to sell the furniture, but at that Allie cried out at last. "You're going to have people we don't even know sitting in our chairs and sleeping in our beds!" So the things were not sold, but instead everything was cleaned and covered with sheets, so that the house appeared to be haunted by large, strangely shaped ghosts.

Allie and Gertrude and Mother spent their last night in Grandma's house. The girls slept in the spool bed under quilts that Grandma had made when she was a young wife. Allie could not think of the leavetaking that would happen tomorrow, or of the future stretching ahead so blank and strange, so she thought instead of Papa. The bed had been his when he was a boy.

Thirteen

Allie looked back as the carriage went down the lane. Grandma was standing beside the gate with the patient Rags beside her. She was wearing the good shawl—the one that Allie had worn on that trip to Canso. It seemed so long ago. Did Grandma remember? Perhaps not. Perhaps she was thinking only of the many partings which she had known in her life.

Allie waved. Gertrude did too, and Grandma waved back. Then there was the bend in the lane and Grandma was gone, and so was the place where they had always lived.

Uncle Matt was driving. He had worked hard to help Mother settle their affairs, and so had Uncle Hugh. Whatever they thought about Mother's decisions, they said little, for it was plain to all of them that Mother would have her way.

Gertrude put her hand into Allie's, and Allie saw that her face was pinched and white. Neither of them spoke until they were at the courthouse in Guysborough, where the coach was waiting. Even then Allie did not speak, for there were no words that seemed right. She stood and took one last long look at the bay. It was gray under a gray sky, and the wind was biting cold. When she had looked her fill, Allie hugged Uncle Matt and got into the coach. Gertrude announced with loud defiance that she was coming back, see if she didn't. Mother kissed Matt on the cheek. Then she got in and the door was closed on them. The driver shouted at the horses and they jolted off.

Then there was the long, bitter cold journey to the train, and the long, grinding, swaying journey on the train. They ate from the basket Mother had packed, and they watched the countryside speed past the windows. Allie slept once and dreamed that she was in the dory, but Papa was not there. She was alone, struggling with the oars, and the sea was rushing at her, ready to sweep over her.

Allie started awake. She did not sleep again, but sat looking out at the woods where the trees were naked against the sky. Now and then there was a town, and then the town would be gone and there would be more woods.

It was night when they came to Montreal, where there were more people and more bustle than Gertrude and Allie had seen in all their lives. Then there was another train, more elegant than the first one. They sat on green plush seats which had crisp white towels over the backs. Gertrude put her head in Allie's lap, tucked her feet under her, and went to sleep as Montreal began to glide past the train windows. At first there were lights, but then there were none and the darkness was a solid wall outside. Allie saw her own reflection in the glass, and her mother's. Mother was asleep.

Allie sat in a daze of fatigue and watched the other passengers doze and nod. Now and then the conductor in his uniform went up and down the aisle. He always smiled at Allie as he passed. Allie's leg grew numb where Gertrude rested, but Allie did not move. At last her eyes closed despite her fear of the dory and the hungry sea. She slept briefly, until her head fell to one side with such a sudden motion that it roused her. But she slept again, and when she woke there was light outside, and there were towns. Allie thought they must be near the end of their journey.

The city of Boston did not suddenly appear. It grew up gradually beside the tracks. First there were small houses. Then the houses were larger and there were more of them. Then there were brick buildings with wintry streets between them. There were horses straining to pull wagons and people plodding through the slush, lifting heavy feet in clumsy overshoes.

The train slowed and Gertrude woke at last. She sat up and looked out at the gray clouds and the gray streets and the buildings where lights burned in the windows even though it was nearly ten in the morning. "I am not going to like it," she said.

Mother was awake and was looking at a little glass she had taken from her valise. She said "Hush! You haven't seen it yet."

"I've seen all I want to," said Gertrude. "I want to go home."

"Hush!" said Mother again.

They clanked and rattled across switchpoints, then glided into the shadows of a great station.

"Boston!" shouted the conductor. "Boston!"

"Susan will meet us," said Mother, and for the first time since Papa's death there was a lift to her voice. "Put your hat on, Allie. And come here, Gertrude. Let me comb your hair. Good heavens!"

It was as if they were back in the kitchen again, with Mother struggling to get Gertrude in order before Papa came home.

Allie put on her hat and wondered if she would know Aunt Susan when they saw her. Aunt Susan had come to the farm once when Allie had been very small. Allie remembered that she had come down to breakfast in a white lawn dressing gown with red ribbons. Allie remembered that, but not much more. A photograph of Aunt Susan had stood on a table in the parlor, but in the picture Aunt Susan had a fixed smile and an ageless, lifeless look, as if she were a person carved from wax. Allie knew that Susan must have more animation than that, for she had gone from Antigonish to Boston as a young girl, and had been a maid to one of the great ladies of Boston. Then she had become a dressmaker. She sewed elegant clothes and Mother believed she had great style.

The train stopped at last, and Mother stood up and began to pull bags and parcels from the rack overhead. Allie took some parcels and Gertrude held fast to her satchel. They stood in the aisle and were jostled by other passengers as they inched their way to the end of the car. When they finally climbed down the steps to the station platform, they were jostled again toward gates made of great iron spikes.

Someone called, "Nell! Nell!"

Allie knew it had to be Aunt Susan who held out her arms to Mother. They hugged. Then Mother cried and so did Aunt Susan.

Susan turned to the girls, and Gertrude stared and pressed close to Allie. Allie remembered the lady in the white dressing gown. That lady had been tall. This one was hardly as tall as Allie. But if she was small, she had a finished look. It was the look of a china figurine with each part of her agreeing most surely with every other part. She wore a gray broadcloth skirt and a short jacket with very large sleeves. Her head supported a great deal of hair and an overwhelming hat, but she was not overwhelmed. Even the big hat looked just as it should.

Allie felt lumpy and mussy. She knew that she smelled of sweat and the peculiar sourness of the railway car. She backed away from her aunt and watched Susan kiss Gertrude, who was too weary to protest or to respond.

Susan turned away and made a small gesture with one hand. Instantly there was a porter. She gave orders in a quiet voice, and the porter took the bags and the parcels and staggered along behind them as they crossed the station.

When they reached the street Susan beckoned again, and there was a carriage. It was driven by a man with a very red nose, and it was drawn by a villainous-looking horse with knobby knees and bald patches on its coat. Everyone got in, and Allie was grateful that this was the last leg of their weary journey. The porter piled parcels around their feet, and Susan opened her purse and gave him something that made him smile. Then the driver clucked to the horse, and they lurched away from the station.

Fourteen

"Dear Grandma," Allie wrote. "We have been here three weeks. It is very nice but we miss you."

"You're supposed to put the date at the top," said Gertrude. She was hanging over the back of Allie's chair, leaning so close that Allie could hear her breathe.

Allie wrote the date, January 2, 1903. Then she went on with the letter.

"Aunt Susan lives in part of a house. Her part is called a flat. It is all on one floor. There is a parlor and a sewing room, and Gertrude and I sleep in the sewing room. There is a bedroom too. In the kitchen there are faucets. When Aunt Susan lights the gas under the boiler she can make the water hot in the tank, and the hot water runs out of one of the faucets. We can have a bath every day if we like. There is a real bathroom and the hot water runs there too."

141

"Tell her about the ice man," said Gertrude.

"It's my letter," Allie declared. "I'll tell her what I want to."

Allie wrote, "There is a man who comes twice a week with ice. He puts it in the ice chest in the kitchen, and we keep the food there. There is a milkman too. He brings milk. There is a boy who brings a newspaper every morning. He comes before it is even light. And there is a boy who comes from the grocer with food."

Allie stopped, overwhelmed by the number of men and boys who served her aunt.

Gertrude said, "Tell her about school."

Allie took a minute to think about that, then began to write again: "We start school tomorrow. It is a big school and it is four streets away. Mother took us to be entered and we met the principal. She is like the head teacher. She was cross because we do not have certificates that say we were born, but she decided to let us in anyway. I will be in the eighth grade and Gertrude will be in the fifth grade."

Allie stopped writing. She felt depressed when she thought of the meeting with the principal of the Cobbett Avenue School. The lady was named Miss Finnegan, and she had dusty hair and wore eyeglasses that pinched the flesh on her nose into a bump. She had asked Gertrude if she knew where the Volga River was. Gertrude did not. Miss Finnegan scowled and asked Allie what she knew about the Dred Scott Decision. Allie had not heard of it.

"I suppose it is foolish to expect her to know much about the history of the United States," said Miss Finnegan to Mother. Miss Finnegan spoke over Allie's head, ignoring

Allie the way Aunt Nonie had always ignored her. "We will expect the girls to catch up with their classmates. I'll have a list of readings made up for them."

Miss Finnegan looked at Allie as if Allie were some farm animal she considered buying. "Twelve years old," she said. "She's the right age for the eighth grade. We can start her there and see how she makes out. Gertrude can go into the fifth grade."

Allie and Gertrude had never been separated before. The thought of that separation dampened Allie's spirits still more.

"There are three hundred pupils at the school," she wrote to Grandma. "That is why we will be in different classes."

She stopped again, and Gertrude said, "You don't have to tell her everything today. You can write again next week."

Allie nodded. "I will send another letter next week," she wrote.

"Now I'll write love," said Gertrude. She took the letter and wrote, "I love you. This is me. Gertrude."

Allie added her own love, signed the letter and folded it. She slipped it into an envelope from Aunt Susan's desk and addressed it to Mrs. Hugh Hughes, Guysborough Intervale, Nova Scotia. There were stamps in a little drawer in the desk, and she put one on the letter. Then she and Gertrude put on their coats and hats and the new galoshes which Susan had bought for them. They went out to the bleak, gray street that was filled with slushy puddles. There was a postbox at the corner, and they mailed Grandma's letter. Then, since there was no one at home and no need for them to be there, they set out down the street, bound for a place called Darling's Tea Room.

"Do you suppose it's owned by somebody named Darling?" said Gertrude.

"I don't think anybody's named Darling," replied Allie. "It's a made-up name."

The shop had a window where plates of fancy iced cakes were on display. Allie and Gertrude had passed by dozens of times as they wandered in the neighborhood, and the sight of the cakes had aroused vivid longing.

"Allie, they must cost a lot," said Gertrude now. Aunt Susan had given them some money, but not much.

"If we don't have enough to buy anything, we'll say we're just looking," said Allie. She had heard Aunt Susan use that phrase in a hatshop on Beacon Street. It had turned out to be a most useful phrase, for it held the salesperson at bay.

Allie opened the door of Darling's Tea Room. She smelled warm, sugary smells and heard a bell jingle. A young woman came from the back and looked over the top of a high glass case.

"Can I help you?" she said, and she smiled. Then she moved from behind the case to a lower counter that had a marble top. Allie saw that she was not really a young woman, but was instead no older than Allie herself. She had smooth, very black hair that she wore in two thick braids. She had very dark eyes and heavy eyebrows, and in spite of her youth, she had a bosom. It swelled proudly under her white shirtwaist.

"Can I help you?" she said again.

Allie smiled, feeling spindly and immature.

"How much are the little cakes in the window?" asked Gertrude.

But then Gertrude spied the glass case where candies were mounded neatly on glass plates. There were heaps of peppermints and piles of lemon drops. There were chocolates and green, brittle-looking candies, and candies like orange jelly. There were tiny, heart-shaped sugar candies with pink writing on them. The writing was about love and kisses.

"How much are those?" Gertrude pointed at the sugar candies.

"Two for a penny."

Gertrude bought two, and a little cake as well. Allie took two chocolates, and the girl with the bosom put the candies into a sack and handed the sack to Allie. Then she blushed and said, "You're the girls from Canada, aren't you? You're going to go to the Cobbett Avenue School. I go there too, and today Miss Finnegan came to our class and talked about you."

"Talked about us?" exclaimed Gertrude. "What did she say?"

"She said . . . she said we're supposed to be nice to you."

There was a moment of shocked silence. Then Gertrude warned, "You'd better be nice!"

She was angry, and the girl drew back. "I'm sorry. I . . . It was dumb for me to say that. I didn't mean . . . I meant, you're new and . . ."

She floundered into silence and then turned to Allie, who was not glaring nearly as savagely as Gertrude. "My name is Rosa, and you'll be in my class."

Allie said, "Oh," and then did not know what else to say.

A large, mustached man came from the back of the shop. Rosa turned to him with obvious relief. "This is my papa, Mr. Raffatini. Papa, these are the girls from Canada. You remember I told you about them?"

Mr. Raffatini's face was very round and his chin almost hid his collar, but he looked pleasant. He beamed at Allie and Gertrude. Allie smiled back at him, but Gertrude continued to glare.

"Are you going out, Rosa?" he said. "Go on, go with your friends."

Rosa looked at Allie, and the look was a plea. "Could I go with you? Just for a little while?"

Allie was puzzled. Why did Rosa want to walk in the snowy streets with them? They really didn't know one another. But perhaps Rosa was only trying to be nice, as Miss Finnegan had commanded. Allie did not want anyone to be forced to treat her kindly, but she did not want to make an enemy either.

"We're not going any place special," she said, "but you can walk along with us if you like."

Rosa ran to get a coat and galoshes. She got more candy too, and carried it along in a little sack. That softened Gertrude considerably. They went out into the street, with Rosa walking so close that she brushed Allie's arm.

146

"If you like," said Rosa, "you can walk to school with me tomorrow. I'll show you where we line up for class."

"That would be nice," replied Allie politely.

"We can go from my house," said Rosa. "If you come by at half past eight, we'll be in plenty of time."

She showed Allie and Gertrude where she lived. It was in a tall brick house around the corner from the tea shop— a place with a high front stoop and narrow, high windows.

"I'll wait for you on the porch tomorrow," she promised.

The three of them wandered on, aimlessly looking into the windows of hardware stores and groceries and toy shops. Rosa talked on and on in her soft voice. She told about her oldest sister who was married and lived in Roxbury and had a baby. Her next sister worked in a shirtwaist factory, a few streets away. Rosa also had two little brothers. They were rough and noisy. She called them pests.

When she had finished with her family, she talked about the school. "You can eat lunch with me tomorrow if you like," she said. "We eat in the basement when we don't want to go home."

"In the basement?" echoed Gertrude. "But a basement is the same as a cellar, isn't it? You mean we're supposed to eat in the cellar?"

Rosa looked fearful. "It's . . . it's not really a cellar. Not at school. It's big and it's got a cement floor and windows. It's the basement and that's different. It's all right, I guess. I eat there. It's easier than going home. I make my sandwich the night before and put it in my lunch box, and . . ."

"Lunch box?" Gertrude echoed the words.

"Yes."

There was a dreadful pause. Then Rosa said, "Yes. It's a . . . a lunch box."

She looked as if she might cry. Allie wondered if she regretted her offer to guide them through their first day in the new school.

"You have a special box to put your sandwich in?" said Gertrude.

"Yes. Well, everyone does and . . . I mean, I do, but . . . but some kids don't. Some kids bring their lunch in a paper sack. You don't really have to have a lunch box. It's all right to use a paper sack."

There was another wretched silence. Rosa stopped in the middle of the sidewalk and gave up her attempt to cope with Allie and Gertrude. "Look, I'll wait for you tomorrow," she said. "You come by my house, and I'll be waiting so . . . so don't forget."

"We won't forget," said Allie.

Rosa turned and ran back toward the tea shop. Just before she got there she looked around and waved. Then she disappeared into the shop.

"A special box to bring your lunch?" Gertrude looked stunned. "That's dumb!"

Allie thought it was dumb too, but she knew from the way Rosa had spoken that a lunch box was a thing you were supposed to have. If you did not have a lunch box, you were somehow deprived and looked down on, like the poor little Collins boy at home who had to wear his big sister's shoes to school.

Allie and Gertrude trudged home, their candies eaten.

Allie wondered how much a lunch box might cost. Not that it mattered. She had no money.

Gertrude said, "Lunch box!" just as they reached the street where Aunt Susan lived. She sounded scornful, but also despairing.

"We don't really have to have one," said Allie. "Rosa said some of the pupils don't have them."

"The poor ones," said Gertrude. "Allie, are we poor? If we ask Mother to buy lunch boxes, would that be so terrible?"

"Why do you care so much?" cried Allie. "You said yourself, a lunch box is dumb!" Suddenly she resented Gertrude, who always looked to her to fix things or explain things. But then Allie found herself resenting many things these days. She resented Miss Finnegan and her question about the Dred Scott Decision. She thought that probably she would not like the Cobbett Avenue School. She resented Mother and her talk of being poor and the way she looked through them as though they were not there. And she had a vague feeling that she might soon resent Rosa. Rosa was trying too hard to be friends, and that made Allie suspicious.

"You never cared about a thing like a lunch box before," she said now.

"Nobody else did either," said Gertrude.

That was it of course. At home they were the Hughes girls. They knew so well who they were and what they were doing that there was no need even to think about it. Here they were strangers in a strange place, and of course Gertrude felt it.

"We aren't poor," said Allie, trying to put some limits on what was wrong. "Mr. Jensen is sending the money for the sawmill, and Mother got money for selling the horses. And there are the island rents. I don't think it's the money that scares Mother. It's not having Papa."

Having said that, Allie knew it was true. Without Papa no amount of money would ever be enough for Mother. Without Papa she would always feel afraid, and she would complain that they could not afford things. She would worry about the future.

But there was no use talking of it. Papa was gone and nothing could bring him back. Yet there were still times when Mother would not believe it. Allie had seen this. She had seen her mother hurry to overtake someone who walked the way Papa had walked, or who held his head the way Papa had held his. It was always a stranger who looked back at Mother, and always she shrank and hurried on, staring in front of her.

"Come on," Allie said. "It will be dark soon. Mother doesn't want us out after dark."

They walked the rest of the way without talking, and when they opened the door to Aunt Susan's vestibule, they saw a light at the top of the stairs. Aunt Susan had heard them coming and had opened the door for them. She waited with threads clinging to her skirt and pins stuck into the front of her shirtwaist. She did not hug them because of the pins, but she smiled.

"Your mother isn't home yet. Come and see what I got for you. I was in Mrs. Peabody's shop today and her little girl goes to the Cobbett Avenue School, and she said all the children there have lunch boxes. So I bought lunch boxes for you. I know you'll think they're silly, but if they're what you should have—well, you should have them."

They were square little tin boxes, each with a handle. Aunt Susan had unwrapped them and set them out on the table. "Do you suppose they're the right kind?"

Allie had never seen a lunch box in her life. She had no idea whether they were the kind the other children took to school or not. What she did know was that Aunt Susan was careful and kind, and that she loved her. "Thank you," she said, wanting to say something more to show that she was truly grateful, but not being able to think of anything more.

"You're very welcome," said Aunt Susan.

Gertrude hugged her, pins and all.

"My word!" she said. "It isn't such a big matter, is it?" And she went back to her sewing, smiling a little as she did so.

Fifteen

The schoolyard had been empty the day Allie and Gertrude had had their interview with Miss Finnegan. It was not empty now. It was alive with boys who ran and slid and jostled one another, and girls who clustered in groups and talked or played quieter games.

"We won't have to be out here long," said Rosa. "The janitor opens the side door early when the weather's cold, and we wait inside for school to start."

She had hardly explained this when a door did open. A thin, gray-faced man looked out of the ugly yellow brick building. From his expression Allie guessed that he did not approve of boys and girls. He did not linger, but propped the door open with a wooden wedge and disappeared back into the building.

There was a surge toward the doorway as pupils stampeded through. Allie and Gertrude followed Rosa into the building and down a short flight of stairs to a dusty, echoing place with a cement floor.

"This is the cellar, isn't it?" said Gertrude.

"It's the basement," Rosa corrected her. She had to shout to be heard above the noise.

Gertrude stood close to Allie while all around boys in knee pants and heavy jackets raced and shouted. At home in Guysborough Mr. Blanchard would never have tolerated the noise, but at home there were not so many pupils. Perhaps when boys and girls came in such overwhelming numbers, thought Allie, teachers could not tame them so easily. Or perhaps the teachers grew weary of trying to quiet them and pretended not to notice the noise.

A short, red-haired boy darted past Gertrude and struck her sharply on the arm.

Gertrude had been bewildered and cowed. Instantly she was furious. She had fought in the schoolyard at home once or twice—fought until Mr. Blanchard came running to stop her. She was ready to fight now. She started after the boy who had struck her.

Allie caught hold of her coat. "Don't!" she warned. "Let him go! Who cares?"

Gertrude tried to wriggle out of the coat. Then she quieted. "Why did he do that?" she said. "I don't even know him."

She looked at Rosa, and Rosa shrugged. "You're new."

But now the boy was running at Gertrude again, grinning, a fist raised as if to strike. At the last second he didn't strike, but skipped past Gertrude without touching her.

Gertrude and Allie watched him. He looked wiry and wicked and one of his front teeth was broken. He whispered something to another boy, and then both boys looked toward Gertrude. Their eyes sparkled with mischief. A third boy joined the first two, and then another came, and another. Then the knot of whispering, jeering boys broke, and Allie and Gertrude and Rosa were surrounded.

"Hey, guinea!" taunted one. He took hold of Rosa's braid and yanked. "Who're your friends, guinea?"

Rosa's expression was grim. She pretended not to notice the tug on her hair, even though it must have hurt.

"Guinea!" A second boy took up the taunt. He tried to pull her hair but she dodged backward. "Hey, guinea!" he yelled, and raced off across the basement. For the moment, the boys seemed to lose interest in tormenting Rosa and the two newcomers.

"What's a guinea?" asked Gertrude.

"It's a bad word," said Rosa. "It means Italian, that's all. Some kids don't like Italians."

Suddenly Allie knew why Rosa was so anxious to be her friend. Rosa had no other friends. Allie looked around and did not see another boy or girl who was as dark-eyed and dark-haired as Rosa, except for Rosa's two little brothers, who were off in a corner by themselves, pretending not to know their sister. In that school Rosa was an outcast. She wanted Allie and Gertrude to be under obligation to her before they discovered this.

Allie's first impulse was to cry out, "You tricked us!" But she didn't cry out. She knew in her heart that she might have done the same thing had she been Rosa.

She had no time to think more about it, for a whistle blew. Miss Finnegan was standing at the top of the stairs with her bosom thrust out and her eyes glittering behind her spectacles.

The tumult in the basement became a shade less deafening. The pupils of the Cobbett Avenue School began to sort themselves into classes.

"The fifth grade is over there," said Rosa. She pushed Gertrude toward a cluster of boys and girls who were trying to line up near the wall.

Gertrude went grudgingly and took a place near the head of the line. She did not stay there. Smaller children elbowed her aside and jostled her down the line. She wound up next to a flaxen-haired girl who had a round, pale face and prominent blue eyes.

The whistle sounded again. Rosa and Allie took places in the eighth grade line. The talking and shuffling stopped. There was quiet in the basement. Into that quiet came the flaxen-haired girl's question to Gertrude.

"You're the kid from Canada, ain't you? You speak English?"

"That's dumb!" scoffed Gertrude.

Miss Finnegan blew her whistle again. "There will be no talking after the whistle blows! Now if we're ready, we'll salute the flag."

Two boys came from the hallway behind Miss Finnegan. One carried the flag, and the second one kept his eyes fixed on Miss Finnegan. When she turned toward the flag he stiffened to attention. Her hand went up to her heart in a salute. He saluted.

Some two hundred and eighty pupils in the basement saluted. "*I pledge allegiance*," said two hundred and eighty voices, male and female, soft and loud, "*to the flag of the United States of America* . . ."

Rosa, saluting, darted a glance at Allie. Allie's hands were at her sides. She had considered saluting for an instant, wondering if Papa would have pledged allegiance to this flag. She decided he would not have done so, not even to be polite. How could he? He was a Canadian. So was Allie. So she did not salute.

Gertrude saw that Allie stood with her hands at her sides, and she did not salute either.

"*. . . and to the republic for which it stands* . . ."

The flaxen-haired girl poked Gertrude with her elbow.

"*. . . one nation, indivisible* . . ."

The boy behind Gertrude shoved, and Gertrude lurched forward. She whirled and glared at the boy. His foot moved. Allie saw the toe of a rubber boot connect with Gertrude's ankle. Gertrude swung a fist and caught the boy a wallop on the side of the head.

"Hey!" he yelled.

The pledge of allegiance faltered and stopped.

Gertrude and the boy were locked in combat. The boy stumbled backward, tripped, and went down. Gertrude threw herself on top of him, pounding at him, while he held his arms up to protect himself.

"Gertrude, don't!" shouted Allie. She ran.

Before she could reach Gertrude two more boys were in the fight. Then Allie was fighting too. She shouted and struck out, enjoying the surge of rage that swept over her.

She felt someone's hair in her hand and she yanked. She heard screams and she was glad. A fist smashed above the bridge of her nose and pain was an exploding light, and then there was a hand across her mouth. She bit. Someone screamed again, and Allie laughed a wicked laugh. Then she was flailing wildly, striking at the boys who crowded around, and at the sea that had taken Papa. And she screamed her rage at Mother, too—Mother who had taken her so far away from home.

Then the battle was over. The boys were scattering, stumbling, scrambling to get away, and Allie was holding fast to Gertrude, who had a piece of someone's collar in her fist.

Miss Finnegan stalked toward them. Two other women marched behind Miss Finnegan, and they twisted their hands with anxiety and looked at Allie and Gertrude in a fearful, stunned way.

"You will go to the office!" said Miss Finnegan. She was shaking with rage.

Gertrude and Allie went, with Miss Finnegan and her aides driving them up the stairs like sheep and down a dingy, green-painted hall to the principal's office. The three boys who had been first to attack came along behind and grouped themselves some distance from Allie and Gertrude. The two women who seemed to feel that they were Miss Finnegan's bodyguards took positions behind the principal's chair.

"Well!" said Miss Finnegan.

"I didn't do anything!" said the boy who had first shoved Gertrude. He was grimy, and his red hair hung over his face like some sort of roof. Allie saw that he was the one who had lost his collar. She was glad. It was only a pity Gertrude had not snatched off his ears.

"He pushed me!" cried Gertrude. "He tried to knock me down. Then he kicked me, and then . . ."

"Quiet!" shouted Miss Finnegan.

"She wouldn't salute the flag," said the boy.

"Gertrude Hughes is a Canadian," said Miss Finnegan. She was so breathless with anger that she could scarcely get out a whole sentence. "Haven't you thought . . . that a Canadian . . . might not wish to salute our flag?"

"No?" croaked the boy. He looked at Allie and Gertrude as if they had warts.

"No," said Miss Finnegan.

"She fights dirty," said another boy. He pointed at Allie. "She bites."

Miss Finnegan pursed her lips and shook her head as if to announce that she would not try to sort out the right and the wrong in this situation. "We must consider this incident closed," she said. "You boys, go to your classrooms. In the future, don't you dare try to correct your classmates! Your teachers can take care of any correction that is needed—or I can."

The boys shuffled out, sending sideways looks at Allie and Gertrude as they went.

Gertrude put out her tongue at them.

"That will do, Gertrude," warned Miss Finnegan. "We've had enough for one morning."

She sat down behind her desk and began to speak slowly and deliberately. "Girls, I know that you have other loyalties. I regret this extremely. But try to understand that Boston is the cradle of liberty, and your schoolmates are proud of this heritage."

"They aren't!" cried Gertrude. "They're bullies! They only wanted an excuse to . . ."

"That will do, Gertrude!" said Miss Finnegan.

"But they . . ."

"I said that will *do*!"

Allie took hold of Gertrude's arm, and Gertrude was still.

"I'm afraid you've gotten off to a bad start," Miss Finnegan continued. "You must try to overcome it. In the future you will report the incident to me if you feel that your schoolmates . . . uh . . . if they don't understand your position. Young people may be . . . uh . . . lacking in judgement, and if they think their institutions are being slighted, they can behave rashly. Now I will take you both to your classrooms, and I do not want to hear ever again that you . . . you . . ."

She paused and groped for a word, breathing out through her nose, for all the world the way Maude breathed out after she got the buggy safely up the lane.

Allie smiled. She tried not to, but she couldn't help it.

"I'm glad that you're amused," said Miss Finnegan. "I wouldn't have suspected that you were insolent, Mary Alice Hughes. Or a bully. You attacked children who are younger and smaller than yourself. Shame! And I'm astonished that you would fight. Ladies do not fight."

"There were three of them," said Allie. "They were . . ."

"Hold your tongue!" cried Miss Finnegan. "If I hear one more word you'll be sent home!"

Allie clenched her teeth. She felt the same rage she had felt during the battle. If Papa were alive this woman would not speak so.

"You don't have to send me home," Allie heard herself say. The words surprised even her. "I'll go by myself."

"I'll go too," said Gertrude.

They went out of the office and down the hall. Miss Finnegan called after them, but they did not stop. The thin gray man who had opened the side door that morning stepped in their way, but they dodged around him. Then they were out the front door and down the stone steps and away.

Sixteen

"Good heavens!" said Mother. She went to the kitchen and got a wet towel to put on Gertrude's forehead where a purple lump was blooming. She listened to Gertrude's confused, tearful account of the battle at the school.

"You've made a great beginning," she said. "Fighting! I suppose you called your schoolmates rebels. And acted as if you were greatly superior because you are Hugheses and you were born on land that came from good King George!"

Allie felt outrage again. "Mother, it wasn't like that! Gertrude didn't call them rebels! And they started it. They tried to push her down and they kicked her just because she didn't salute their flag. And there were three to one, and . . ."

"And you had to pitch in on the side of honor and good King George," said Mother. "King George has been in his grave for a hundred years. Now listen to me. You must go back to school. I'll go with you and talk to Miss Finnegan, but you must go back."

"I won't go!" declared Gertrude.

"You will," insisted Mother, "and you will try to get along. And if the other children tease you, you will pretend you don't notice. They'll soon grow tired of it. Get yourselves to rights now. Hurry up!"

There was no help for it. They washed their faces and combed their hair and brushed the dust off their clothes. Then they followed Mother back to the Cobbett Avenue School and straight to Miss Finnegan's office. Allie marched in and faced the principal with her chin high and her teeth clenched to keep her lips from trembling. She quickly learned that if fighting during the morning assembly was disgraceful, marching out of school without permission was absolutely criminal.

"We cannot have that sort of behavior!" declared Miss Finnegan. Her spectacles vibrated on her nose. "I cannot take the responsibility for pupils who may walk away at any time and take to the highways and the byways. If it happens again, they will be expelled."

Allie wanted to say that they had not taken to the highways and the byways, but had gone straight home. Miss Finnegan would surely feel that this was insolence, however, so she held her tongue.

"I've talked with the girls," said Mother. "It won't happen again." She straightened in her chair so that she was as upright as Miss Finnegan. "I do understand your position, but you must understand that they don't want to salute the United States flag. I don't know how you plan to explain this to the other children, but you simply must find a way to do it."

"We will manage," said Miss Finnegan.

The conversation reminded Allie of some of the conversations between Grandma and Mother. Both sides always won a little.

Mother left then, and Allie and Gertrude had to go to their classrooms. Miss Finnegan led the way, and they came to the fifth grade first. Gertrude was marched into the room while Allie waited in the hall. Allie saw desks and chairs that were fastened to the floor, and rows of boys and girls who stared at Gertrude while Miss Finnegan exchanged a few words with Gertrude's teacher. Then the principal came out and marched Allie to the eighth grade room. She opened the door and gestured for Allie to go in. Then she closed the door, and Allie was staring at thirty-one pupils and at a teacher who was young and very thin, and who had a round, plain face.

The teacher's name was Miss Spencer. She did not appear overjoyed to have Allie in her class, but she did not seem actively spiteful either. She simply told Allie to take a seat in the second row and informed her that the class was reviewing compound fractions. "Open your copybook and write down the examples you see on the board," she said.

Allie was swept by despair. She knew nothing about compound fractions and she could not imagine what one did with them. She wrote down the numbers that were on the blackboard, but she did it with dull hopelessness. She did not understand and she could never understand and she knew it. She would not care. She would simply endure.

The other pupils answered questions. When Allie was called on she did not even try. "I don't know," was all she said. Miss Spencer went briskly on to the next pupil, leaving Allie to sit in dumb agony.

After arithmetic there was history, and that was no better. Miss Spencer asked questions about the Monroe Doctrine. The other boys and girls could answer. Allie surely could not.

Noon came at last, and Allie and Gertrude crouched with Rosa on a bench in the basement. At first the noise was not as deafening as it had been that morning, mainly because the pupils were all eating. When the last sandwich had been consumed, however, the noise level went up again. The younger boys played tag. The girls gossiped. Allie watched, not thinking, not letting herself feel anything.

But then a group of girls strolled past Rosa. They glanced her way and one of them waved a handkerchief in front of her nose as if she smelled something strange.

"Rosa, what's the price of olive oil these days?" called the girl. "It smells so strong today!"

"How much you pay for macaroni, Rosa?" taunted a second girl. "You've got to eat a lot of macaroni to get so fat, don't you?"

Rosa flushed scarlet, but she said nothing.

"Fat?" cried Gertrude. "You're not fat, Rosa."

"I hate them!" said Allie. She had forgiven Rosa for maneuvering her into friendship. Rosa at least behaved like a human being. The others were savages. And if Mother believed these boys and girls would tire of their teasing, she was greatly mistaken. They had surely not tired of teasing Rosa.

"Don't pay any attention," said Rosa. "My mother says we should feel sorry for them. They're so . . . so dumb that they don't understand anybody who isn't just like them."

"Dumb," echoed Gertrude. It was now her favorite word. "Dumb, dumb, dumb!"

The boy who had shoved Gertrude that morning began to approach. Gertrude glared at him and stood up, and he veered away toward a group of boys and did not look back. Gertrude sat down again.

The whistle blew and lines formed to march back to the classrooms. The afternoon session began. In Allie's class there was geography and spelling and Allie began to take heart. She spelled "meridian" after two other pupils failed, and she knew that the Grand Banks were an undersea plateau near Newfoundland. Any child in Nova Scotia knew this!

At three o'clock Allie was not dismissed with the rest of the class. Miss Finnegan had decreed that for a month the Hughes girls would remain for an extra half-hour. They were to do penance for the insurrection of the morning.

"You can wash the blackboard," said Miss Spencer to Allie.

Washing the blackboard turned out to be the most pleasant event of the day. Allie cleaned the board with an eraser, then got water from a smelly little closet near the stairs and washed the board with a rag. The slate was marvelously black when it was wet, and hardly less black when it had dried clean and smooth.

When she finished with the blackboard, Allie filled Miss Spencer's inkwell and watered the plants on the windowsill. It was quiet and friendly with just herself and Miss Spencer in the room, and Miss Spencer smiling as she watched Allie move about. When the half-hour was over Miss Spencer and Allie went down the hall to the stairs and down the stairs to the side door. Gertrude was waiting in the schoolyard with her teacher, and the teachers watched Allie and Gertrude set out for home.

Rosa was hovering at the corner. "What did she make you do, Allie?"

"I washed the blackboard. It was all right."

"I read a book," said Gertrude. "It was about Indians."

"Want to come home with me?" asked Rosa.

She was pleading and eager again and they went.

The house where Rosa lived was too warm. It was also dim and Allie thought it had too many chairs and tables. Rosa took them in through the front door to a hall where there was a staircase with lots of red carpeting. Then she led them past the staircase to the back of the house, and there was a big kitchen, which wasn't dim, but was bright and full of dishes and pots and tables with shining bowls. There they met Mrs. Raffatini.

Rosa's mother looked like Rosa, except that of course she was older. She was stouter too, and much more cheery. She asked Allie and Gertrude how they had liked their first day at the school. She did not wait for their answer, but banged pots about and rambled on in a sunny voice about how strange she had felt when first she came to America. She also stoked them with cocoa and stuffed them with sweet cookies, and now and then she went to the kitchen door and called out threats to Rosa's little brothers, who were thumping about upstairs.

It was beginning to be dusk when they left for home, and as they reached the corner of Aunt Susan's street they saw Susan going up the walk to the house. They ran to catch up with her. The first day of school was over and they had survived.

But then there was the next day, and the day after that. Things did not get worse. They could not. But they did not get much better. Allie began to get a grip on fractions, and Gertrude learned quite a lot about Indians, but Allie often saw traces of tears on Gertrude's cheeks when they started home in the afternoons. Once there was a mark under one eye.

"You were fighting again," said Allie.

"Nobody saw," Gertrude told her. "That rotten Murphy kid won't tell because that would make him a tattletale. Besides, he hit me first."

Allie knew that the Murphy boy probably had struck first. She also knew that Miss Finnegan would not think that was a good reason for fighting. Miss Finnegan wanted Allie and Gertrude to speak to her if their schoolmates abused them, but clearly they couldn't. Not without being tattletales themselves.

They had been at the school almost five weeks when

Allie woke one night to find Gertrude tossing wildly and shouting in her sleep. "I'll kill you! You do that and I'll smash you!"

Mother and Aunt Susan came running. They woke Gertrude, but she would not talk to them. After they went back to their own bed Allie said, "What were you dreaming?"

Gertrude had her back turned to Allie. "It was that Murphy kid," she said. "He set this big dog at me, so I was choking him and . . . and then it got all confused."

Neither of them said more, and Gertrude went back to sleep after a while. Allie did not. She lay for the rest of the night feeling a heavy, foreboding feeling.

Each morning Allie and Gertrude went out armored against the outrages of the day. They came home at night somewhat restored by Mrs. Raffatini's cocoa and somewhat comforted by the knowledge that Rosa seemed to admire them. Rosa and the cocoa were better than nothing, but they were not really enough. Allie began to feel that they had lived this way forever, and that the farm in Nova Scotia was a dream that she had dreamed long ago.

Then one night Allie woke into a special stillness, and she knew it must be snowing. She got up and went to the window to look out at the white flakes drifting down around the streetlamp. She went into the hall, intending to go to the bathroom. There was light in the parlor. Mother and Aunt Susan were sitting there talking quietly together.

"It will be perfect, if only I can get it," Allie heard her mother say. "Mrs. Hewitt at the agency said I was the most qualified. She's written to Mr. Reed to tell him as much, so I'm very hopeful. She says Mr. Reed always takes her recommendations as gospel."

Allie peeked through the crack between the door and the jamb. Her aunt was at the table, facing her, and Mother sat with her back to the door.

"Of course nothing will be decided until I go to Manchester to see Mr. Reed," said Mother.

Susan must have glimpsed the white of Allie's nightdress in the hall. "Allie, is that you?" she called.

Allie came around the door. "I got up to go to the bathroom."

"Come and hear your mother's news," Susan said.

Allie thought her mother looked annoyed. Probably Mother had not planned to tell her the news so soon, or she would have spoken of it earlier.

"No real news," said Mother. "Not yet. It's just a chance. I may be employed to manage the household for a gentleman named Reed. It's an elegant establishment, and if I get the position, I'll do the cooking and have all the responsibility for keeping the place in order. There will be a housemaid to see to the dusting and the beds, and a boy to carry the wood and do the scrubbing, and of course I'll supervise them. And a laundress will come in once a week."

"My goodness!" said Allie. It sounded marvelous. Perhaps that was why Mother hadn't said anything. If she told and then didn't get the position, they would all be so disappointed.

"As soon as Mrs. Hewitt hears from Mr. Reed, I'm to go to Manchester to see him. I'll stay the night, or perhaps

169

two nights, and cook dinner and see to the serving. If we are both satisfied, Mr. Reed and I will strike a bargain."

There was a glow in Mother's face. Allie guessed what she was thinking. This person named Reed would be satisfied. Mother knew how things should be done, and any right-thinking person must be pleased with what she did.

"Where will we live if you go?" said Allie. In her mind's eye she pictured a big house. It would have to be big to have so many people in service. Off in some wing of the house there might be a little sitting room for them, and a bedroom where they could sleep together.

But Mother did not answer, and Allie saw some of the glow disappear.

"Mother, where is Manchester?" She felt suddenly as if she had put her foot on the topmost step of a stair, and the step was not there. "Is it far from here?"

"Not too terribly far, Allie. But let's not think too much about it. Nothing is settled yet. Now you'd better get back to bed or there'll be no getting you up in the morning."

Allie nodded. She went to the bathroom and then back to bed, where she lay staring at the ceiling. It was plain to her that Mother had not given a thought to Allie and Gertrude when she spoke to the woman at the employment agency. She had not asked whether there was a place in that great house for the housekeeper's two daughters. She was worried only about the position, and this frightened Allie greatly.

Seventeen

The letter came from Mr. Reed. He was pleased with Mrs. Hewitt's account of Mrs. Hughes. Mrs. Hughes was to journey to Manchester, a distance of some fifty odd miles, to see Mr. Reed, and to be seen by him.

Allie's mother began her preparations. There was much washing and ironing, and there were endless lists of dishes which Mother might cook for Mr. Reed.

"The dinner should be simple, but very good," said Mother. "Clear soup to start, and then fish with a plain white sauce. Then the roast. Do you think pork would be too heavy? Yes, perhaps it would. I'll do lamb so that it's still a bit pink, and serve it with mint jelly and little potatoes. Mrs. Hewitt says Mr. Reed is fond of game. I wonder if one could get wild duck."

"Will Mr. Reed eat all that?" asked Gertrude. She was awed by all the fuss.

"He dines formally every evening," said her mother. "A formal dinner means five courses, and fruit."

She went back to her lists then, and Allie and Gertrude left for school. "We'll be fat as pigs when we go to Manchester," said Gertrude after they reached the street.

Allie said nothing. Her mother might have great plans for Mr. Reed's dinner, but still nothing had been said about how they might live in Manchester. Did Mr. Reed even know that Mrs. Hughes had two daughters?

Allie knew that Aunt Susan was worried too. One day Allie had left Gertrude at Rosa's house. Rosa's younger brothers had started a game of cards with Gertrude, and Gertrude wanted to finish it. And so Allie had come home alone. She had started up the stairs and had heard her mother and Aunt Susan talking. Even though the door at the top of the stairs was closed, she could hear, and what she heard made her stand frozen for a moment.

"If you do care," Aunt Susan said, "it's not plain to see. Is there a place for them in this rich man's house? Did you ask that? Have you given even a thought to it?"

"Susan, you behave as if they're three and need someone to wipe their noses. I'm sure something can be managed. I have to see first if I've got the position."

"You aren't going to see first if there's a way to keep the girls with you?"

"I'm sure there will be," said Mother.

"But Nell . . ."

"I don't want to talk about it now!" Mother's voice was sharp. "Let's not borrow trouble. I can only cope with one thing at a time."

Aunt Susan said no more, and Allie turned and crept back down the stairs. She opened the vestibule door noisily and let it slam, and then she tramped upstairs.

Allie never let Aunt Susan know that she had overheard. She knew there was nothing comforting Susan could say. And she never told Gertrude about it. To Gertrude the house in Manchester meant a release from Cobbett Avenue School. It meant a new adventure in a new place. She was happy for the first time in weeks—in months! Allie could not take that away from her.

The day they left Mother so busy with her lists, Allie decided she herself must stop worrying. It only wearied her to go over and over the possibilities in her mind. She smiled, remembering Grandma. Grandma believed that the Lord gave each one his burdens for each day, and that we only made them heavier if we dragged yesterday's luggage with us, or borrowed some from tomorrow. Allie sometimes thought of the Lord as a very tall man handing out parcels wrapped in brown paper.

But Grandma was right. The burden she carried now belonged to tomorrow. She could not even know the size of it yet, so she must put it out of her mind.

And there was Rosa at the corner. Allie was glad to see her, and glad that she looked unusually pink and excited.

"My Aunt Julie is coming to visit us," said Rosa, as soon as Allie and Gertrude were near enough to talk.

"Your aunt?" said Gertrude. "She's coming from Italy?"

It was a sensible question. All the family stories in the Raffatini house were of Italy. Where else would Rosa have an aunt?

But, "Not from Italy," said Rosa. "From St. Louis. That's a city near the Mississippi River, and it's far away from here."

Gertrude squeezed her eyes shut as if she were picturing a map in her mind. "Oh! The Mississippi. That's the river that runs all the way down the middle of the country."

Rosa nodded. "It will take Aunt Julie two days to come on the train. Papa says she's going to have a drawing room all to herself."

"That's nice," said Allie. She was not sure what a drawing room might be, but it sounded more pleasant than sitting up all night in a coach, as she and Gertrude and Mother had on the way from Nova Scotia.

"Aunt Julie's my papa's older sister," said Rosa. "I guess she's really old. Papa says she was grown up before he was even born. She came to the United States before Papa did and she married an American. Well, he's an American whose father and mother were Italian, but he's an American all the same. He has a factory that makes pocketbooks and wallets and things like that. I think he and Aunt Julie must be rich, because they send wonderful presents at Christmas. She sent me the little gold pin I showed you— the one I keep in the shell box on my dresser. And she sent my China doll."

"Do you play with dolls still?" said Gertrude.

"No. I used to, but I didn't play with that one. It's too beautiful to play with. Mama keeps it in the cupboard in the spare bedroom."

If Gertrude thought that a doll which could not be played with was silly, she was polite enough not to say so. It was obvious that Rosa thought it was wonderful, and that she was looking forward to the visit of this aunt, whom she had never met.

That afternoon the girls found Mrs. Raffatini in a frenzy of preparation. She had all the dishes out of all of the cupboards. Allie and Rosa were put to work washing and drying them while Mrs. Raffatini wiped the cupboard shelves with a damp cloth.

The next day Mrs. Raffatini was ironing sheets when the girls came in from school, and the windows were open in the spare room to air the place out. Allie and Rosa stripped the bed in that room and put on fresh sheets, hurrying because the wind blew in so coldly on them.

The day after that the aunt was there.

"She wants to meet you and Gertrude," said Rosa on the way to school. "I told her you'd come home with me when school is over."

To Allie's surprise, Rosa did not seem really delighted to say this.

"What's your aunt like?" asked Gertrude. "Why does she want to meet us?"

"I don't know why," said Rosa. "Aunt Julie's . . . well, she's old. Yes. And she . . . she's kind of quiet. Maybe she's sort of stern, you know? Like last night it wasn't as if Papa was talking to a sister. He was so respectful, as if she was a customer in his shop. And Mama's so nervous she spilled the gravy on the kitchen floor. I think she wants Aunt Julie to like her, and she isn't sure Aunt Julie does. Aunt Julie's still in bed this morning, and we couldn't even talk at the breakfast table in case we might make some noise and wake her."

Rosa thought about this, her face glum. Allie felt sorry for her. Rosa had so looked forward to this aunt's arrival. Perhaps she imagined that it would be cozy and joyful. Grownups were so seldom joyful, Allie knew, and they often were disappointing.

When they went in through the kitchen door of the Raffatini house that afternoon, Mrs. Raffatini was bustling about fixing a tray. She sent Rosa and Allie and Gertrude to the parlor, a room seldom used by the family. There sat a woman who was certainly much older than Mr. Raffatini, and much, much thinner than Mrs. Raffatini. She had a long face that was handsome without being in the least pretty, and her gray hair was drawn back over her ears and then twisted into a knot at the nape of her neck. Allie saw that the dress the woman wore was gray and plain, but it was fastened at the throat with a heavy gold brooch. Allie suspected that the dress had cost a great deal. The shawl over the woman's shoulders was a richness of red and green and blue, and it looked expensive too, and very soft.

"Aunt Julie, I brought my friends to meet you," said Rosa.

"I see," said Aunt Julie. She did not smile and she did not hold out her hand. She just bent her head slightly. But she looked at them searchingly, and the dark eyes in that long, somewhat yellow face were bright and keen.

"Rosa tells me you are from Canada." She spoke almost

176

without an accent, but there was a certain studied manner to her speech. "You have not been long in Boston, eh?"

"We came in December," replied Allie.

"And how do you like it? " said the aunt, whose name was Mrs. Pelucci.

Allie wondered if Rosa had told about their troubles at school. She felt a pricking of annoyance. Now Mrs. Pelucci might quiz them about their battles with their schoolmates. Grownups could be that way. They would ask about anything.

But when Allie did not answer her immediately, Mrs. Pelucci did not ask any more questions. Instead she began to talk about the troubles anyone might have living in a new place.

"Sometimes people who come from Italy find a way to live so that other Italians are always around them. There are sections in every city where all the shops are kept by Italians, and one can go for weeks without hearing English spoken. It is the same with people who come from Germany. I never think this is a good way to live. If you always speak Italian, you don't learn English so well. But it is not easy to be among strange people even if there is no problem with the language. It takes courage."

Mrs. Pelucci stopped speaking then, for Mrs. Raffatini came in with a tray. There was tea as well as cocoa, and there were the sweet cookies that the girls loved. Mrs. Raffatini sat down to have tea with them that afternoon. It was a thing she had never done before.

She started to speak in a rapid patter of Italian, but Mrs. Pelucci raised a hand to stop her. "English!" she said. "We must speak English always. It is better for the children."

Mrs. Raffatini looked pained, and for a moment her sunny, cheerfulness disappeared. But then she smiled again and said, "What do you think of our Rosa? She is going to be tall like her father."

"Like her grandfather, you mean," said Mrs. Pelucci. "He was so tall, like a tree, with shoulders this broad!"

Rosa smiled and blushed as Mrs. Pelucci held her two hands apart to show what a mighty man her father had been. Mrs. Pelucci's eyes rested on Rosa for a second, and then went to Allie's face. There was something calculating in her look. It made Allie self-conscious.

"You know," Mrs. Pelucci said, "I do not have children, and this is a sadness for me. I think while I am here I will try to know the children of my brother. Saturday we will have an outing. We will see some things in Boston that I have read about, and in the afternoon there is a concert. If you wish, I will be glad to have you, Allie, and you too, Gertrude, come with us."

Rosa smiled her shy smile. "Oh, you can come, can't you? Ask your mother."

"Thank you," said Allie. "I'll ask."

All the sweet cookies were eaten then, and the cocoa was gone. Allie and Gertrude went home. They told Mother and Aunt Susan about Rosa's aunt from St. Louis, and Gertrude said, "She's kind of serious. She's skinny. Not fat like Mrs. Raffatini, and she's not really jolly, but she wants to take us on Saturday when she and Rosa and the

Raffatini boys go out. We're going to look at some things and then go to a concert."

Gertrude had heard about concerts, and she was not sure she would like sitting still for an hour or more while people played music. Just the same, they had not had any outings since they came to Boston, and it would be something different.

But Mother was not interested in Mrs. Pelucci or in concerts either. She was paging through a cookbook and she looked irritated. "We'll see," she said.

"Mother, I think we have to let Mrs. Pelucci know," said Allie. She thought of Mrs. Pelucci reproving Mrs. Raffatini for speaking Italian, and she decided that she would not like it if Mrs. Pelucci reproved her for being rude. She did not know why Mrs. Pelucci wanted them to go on Saturday, or why she had wanted to meet Rosa's friends. She had not known many grownups who were curious about children. Just the same, Mrs. Pelucci was different, and they were Rosa's friends, and Allie wanted to go.

"Well," said Mother. "I don't suppose it would hurt if you went."

But when Saturday morning came, Gertrude was sniffling and coughing, so Allie went alone to the Raffatinis'. She was scrubbed and brushed, and she had a fifty-cent piece which Aunt Susan had given her so that she could pay her share of any expenses.

"Rank extravagance," Mother had said when she saw Aunt Susan give her the money.

Allie hardly heard this remark, for the day stretched ahead filled with adventure and golden with promise.

Rosa and Mrs. Pelucci were ready when Allie arrived at the house. The Pelucci boys were more than ready. They raced up and down the sidewalk, unable to be still.

"Has your aunt had time to show you the North Church?" said Mrs. Pelucci as they started out. "Rosa tells me she works long hours each day making dresses."

Allie shook her head. "No. We haven't seen any church except St. Peter's, where we go to Mass on Sunday."

Mrs. Pelucci smiled. "The North Church is very famous. I am surprised you do not know of it."

"It's the church where Paul Revere watched for the signal that the British were coming," said Rosa. "It's in the poem, you know. 'The Midnight Ride of Paul Revere.'"

Allie looked blank.

"You do not know it?" said Mrs. Pelucci. "Never mind. You will."

They walked to the place where the streetcar stopped. Allie was glad that the day was cold enough so that the snow remained decently in bounds and did not run into puddles on the sidewalk. The sky was very blue, and when Allie took off her mittens she could feel the sun warm on her hands.

When they got to the North Church, it was a disappointment. The walk in front of the place was clear of snow, but it was stained with pigeon droppings. Some of the people who hurried up and down the street looked shabby. Some looked rough. None seemed to care about the fact that the church had played a part in the long-ago war for independence.

Allie looked around. She saw square, ugly buildings crowding in on the old church—buildings that were streaked with soot. "It's dirty," she said, "and it's crowded. But everything here is, isn't it?"

It was an echo of the weariness in her own mind. She was tired of Boston, where the snow was grimy almost as soon as it stopped falling. She was homesick for Guysborough and the gentle slopes where the snow looked clean until it melted away in the spring.

"If this is such an important place," said Allie, "why don't the people keep it cleaner?"

"Because these people are too used to it," said Mrs. Pelucci. "They did not travel far to see it."

They tried the door and it was locked, so they turned away and walked on, with Allie on one side of Mrs. Pelucci and Rosa on the other. The boys dodged and darted about them. Allie felt Mrs. Pelucci's arm under her hand, and it was almost as if she were home again, walking in the lane with Grandma. The instant this thought came to her, Allie regretted it. It made her terribly homesick for Grandma. Besides, Mrs. Pelucci was too tall to be like Grandma, and her voice was too strong, and she was rather distant. Grandma was dear and loving, and Allie missed her terribly.

At a corner Mrs. Pelucci stopped and looked up and down. "I think we cannot walk all morning," she said. "I think before the concert we should stop and have something to eat."

There was a cab clop-clopping along. Mrs. Pelucci put up her hand, and the cabbie stopped.

"You will take us to the Parker House," said Mrs. Pelucci. The cabbie tipped his hat.

Mrs. Pelucci got into the cab, and the two little boys scrambled in and sat across from her. Rosa sat next to them, and Mrs. Pelucci made room for Allie to sit beside her. At the end of the cab ride there was the Parker House, a hotel which Mrs. Pelucci said was a famous Boston institution. They would have their lunch there.

Allie and Rosa were awed by the place, and even the two little boys stopped their shoving and their laughing when they looked around. There was a very high ceiling in the dining room, and a good deal of starch in the tablecloths. The waiters were so stiff that they might have been starched too. Mrs. Pelucci ordered for them all; they had ham, which was very good, and a lettuce salad. Allie was nervous about the salad. It slipped about on the plate so much that she was sure she would send it skidding to the floor every time she put a fork to it. But along with the salad there were soft white rolls which were delicious. They were also easy to eat, and Allie had three.

The waiter made a great fuss about brushing away crumbs when the ham and salad and rolls were finished. Then he brought ice cream in little dishes, and coffee for Mrs. Pelucci.

Mrs. Pelucci drank only half of her coffee. She did not want to linger—possibly because Rosa's two little brothers had gotten over their fit of awe and were kicking each other under the table. After she paid the bill, they went out into the afternoon sunshine, and Mrs. Pelucci wondered if they had enough time to see the Public Gardens before the concert. She decided they did not, and they started to walk again.

They had gone for perhaps two blocks when suddenly Mrs. Pelucci stopped and said, "Eh?"

Allie turned toward her and saw her bending, one hand to her side, her face gray. "Allie! Rosa! I must sit down!"

There was no place to sit but the steps of a building. Allie and Rosa helped her get there, and Rosa's little brothers shuffled beside Rosa with fright in their faces.

"Aunt Julie, what is it?" asked Rosa.

Mrs. Pelucci gestured with one hand, and Allie could not tell whether she meant to reassure them or to tell them that she couldn't speak. She leaned against the wall of the bulding and closed her eyes.

"We'll get Papa!" cried Rosa, seizing Mrs. Pelucci's purse and fumbling for money. "I'll send the boys in a cab!"

"No, Rosa," said Mrs. Pelucci. "It is better now. I will stay here for a minute. Then we will all go home."

She closed her eyes again and leaned against the building.

"I'll get a carriage," said Allie.

She took the purse and ran to the corner. There was a cab there in front of a china shop, but the cabbie said he had promised to wait for a passenger. Allie wondered what Aunt Susan would do if a cabbie refused to come with her, and she decided that Aunt Susan would bribe the man. She opened Mrs. Pelucci's purse and took out a dollar.

"You'll get this and the fare besides if you come," she promised.

"Oh," said the man. "Well, if it's that important."

Allie hopped into the carriage so that the man couldn't get away from her. The horse plodded down the street to the building where Mrs. Pelucci waited, and Allie jumped out. She got under one of Mrs. Pelucci's arms, Rosa got under the other, and the two lifted Mrs. Pelucci up off the steps, groaning and gasping, and helped her across the sidewalk into the cab.

Allie and Rosa got in beside Mrs. Pelucci, and Rosa's little brothers tucked themselves in too.

Mrs. Pelucci moaned each time the carriage jolted over a bump in the street. By the time they reached the lane where the Raffatinis lived, she was so pale that Allie was sweating with fright. Mrs. Raffatini ran out when she saw the cab and sent one little brother racing to get the doctor. The other one went to bring Mr. Raffatini from the shop.

Mrs. Pelucci limped into the house with Mrs. Raffatini on one side and Rosa on the other. Allie paid the cabbie with Mrs. Pelucci's money, then went into the house and sat in the parlor. She saw Mr. Raffatini come from the shop, and she saw the doctor arrive. After the doctor went up the stairs, Rosa came down.

"She keeps moaning and holding her side," said Rosa. "Do you suppose it's her heart? Could she be dying?"

Allie did not want to think of that. If Mrs. Pelucci could be struck down on the street like that, what of Grandma? If she suddenly became ill, there would be no one at the farm to help her. What if she fell in the lane? She would lie where she had fallen, and no one would be the wiser—not for a long time.

Allie closed her eyes and silently thanked the Lord for sending the illness to Rosa's aunt and not to Grandma. Then, since she could not be really sure about Grandma, Allie prayed again, asking the Lord to keep her safe.

Mr. Raffatini and the doctor came downstairs. Mr. Raffatini looked in at Rosa and Allie and smiled. "It will be all right," he said. "It is something about the digestion."

"You mean Aunt Julie just has a stomachache?" said Rosa.

The doctor smiled, showing teeth that were very white and very even. "Not quite so simple," he said. "We can't be sure. A little bilious attack perhaps, but it certainly isn't her heart. I wish mine were half that strong."

He turned to Mr. Raffatini. "She had better stay in bed for a few days. These things often ease themselves with rest and a simple diet. Has she been eating anything rich in the past day or two?"

Rosa told about the ham then, and Allie mentioned the rolls and ice cream. "Ah!" said the doctor. He nodded to Mr. Raffatini. "I've told Mrs. Raffatini—nothing but tea and toast. We'll see. I'll stop back in the morning."

He went out. Allie left soon after, walking home through the sunny winter afternoon. Mother was in the parlor when she came in. "You're home early," she said.

"Mrs. Pelucci wasn't feeling well." Allie did not want to say more about it than that, so she went into the sewing room. Gertrude was still in bed, sleeping, and Allie sat and watched her for a while. She was smiling in her sleep, as if she was dreaming a pleasant dream, and her breathing was clear and even. Allie guessed that her cold must be better, and she was glad.

Eighteen

"I don't see why you have to go there today," said Mother.
"You spent most of yesterday with Rosa Raffatini."

Allie did not want to explain. Mother would have said
it was silly. And Allie did not really understand it herself.
She knew only that she had awakened in the night feeling
anxious about Mrs. Pelucci. Anxious, and a little bit guilty.
She had prayed to the Lord to keep Grandma safe, but
she had not prayed for Mrs. Pelucci. She had been glad
that the illness had come to Mrs. Pelucci instead of to
Grandma, and that was not right. She felt as if she had to
watch over Mrs. Pelucci now, as if she could not protect
Grandma if Mrs. Pelucci was not well. And that was
foolish, for she could not protect Grandma in any event.
Just the same, she had to go to the Raffatinis.

Rosa opened the door for Allie, and when Allie asked

her about Mrs. Pelucci she said, "She's better. She's sitting up. You want to see her?"

Allie did. She followed Rosa up the stairs and into a room where there was a wide bed covered with a green silk spread. Mrs. Pelucci was not in the bed, but in a big armchair that looked as if it had too much stuffing. She wore a dark, heavy-looking dressing gown, and her bony hands were clasped in her lap.

"So, Allie!" she said. "But you are good to come and see me!"

She held out a hand, and when Allie went to her she put the hand on Allie's wrist and looked into Allie's face as if she were searching for something there. Allie dropped her eyes, thinking of her jumbled prayer of the day before. But Mrs. Pelucci could not possibly guess anything of that.

After a moment Mrs. Pelucci let go of Allie's wrist. "Rosa, bring that little chair and put it here," she said.

Rosa brought a small straight chair from the other side of the bed. She put it near Mrs. Pelucci's chair, and Mrs. Pelucci nodded to Allie. "Sit here."

Allie sat, and Rosa sat on the bed, and Mrs. Pelucci smiled at the two of them. The smile was unexpected, and Allie found herself smiling back.

"I gave you a fright, eh? I gave myself a fright too. But today I am better. I had tea and toast and no butter, and Rosa has been with me to keep me company. She tells me about her school where she goes with you. She says she has no friends there but you."

It was true. The other pupils laughed and hurried away when Rosa was near. If some of them did not hurry away, but instead tried to talk to Rosa, she would always lower her eyes and leave as soon as she could. She was fearful of insult, and she would not fight the way Gertrude fought. She seemed to trust only Allie, and having gained Allie's friendship, Rosa now clung to her with an intensity that sometimes made Allie feel trapped. Had Allie made an excuse one day after school and gone straight home instead of stopping at Rosa's for cocoa and cookies, Rosa would have been terribly hurt.

In spite of the clinging, Allie liked Rosa. She was kind and gentle, and she would listen with real interest to Allie's stories of the farm, of Grandma, of the Hughes land that had come into the family so long ago. Allie could not speak yet about Papa, and Rosa did not ask. So it was always comfortable. There was also the admiration that shone in Rosa's face when Allie was with her. How could Allie not like someone who admired her?

Allie felt Mrs. Pelucci's eyes on her and wondered how much of this Mrs. Pelucci guessed. Mrs. Pelucci had that look again, as if she were trying to see into Allie's mind.

"I tell Rosa she must stand up more for herself," said Mrs. Pelucci. "She should not just cry when bad things happen.

"But enough of that. Tell me, Allie, how it is with you at home? Rosa says your mother will go this week to see a rich gentleman who wants a housekeeper. Will Rosa lose her friend soon, do you think?"

Allie did not want to talk of Mr. Reed and Manchester. She did not want Mrs. Pelucci to see her doubts about the future, and about Mother. "I don't know," she said.

"Mother can't be sure about the position until she sees Mr. Reed."

"Let us hope it will be happy for your Mother wherever she goes. And for you." Mrs. Pelucci leaned back in her chair and closed her eyes. The light came slanting across her face so that one half was deeply in shadow. Her eyes looked sunken in and her cheeks hollow.

"Aunt Julie, are you tired?" asked Rosa timidly.

"I should go home," said Allie.

Mrs. Pelucci did not stop her, but she said, "Come and see me again. Perhaps I will be downstairs when you come tomorrow with Rosa. If not, you come up."

Rosa and Allie went out and down the stairs. "Aunt Julie likes you," Rosa confided when they reached the front door. "She was asking all sorts of questions about you this morning."

"Questions?" said Allie. "What questions?"

"Oh, about your aunt, and how big her flat is, and . . . and when your mother is going to Manchester—things like that."

"Oh," said Allie, not knowing what else to say. She went out feeling more unsettled than when she had come. She did not care to have Mrs. Pelucci so interested in her. And yet, she thought, what harm could there be in it?

Allie walked the few blocks to Aunt Susan's, and when she came into the flat she saw the parlor awash with bits and pieces of Mother's clothing. Underdrawers were folded on one chair, petticoats on another. Stockings were paired and rolled into neat balls on the table.

"You're taking all these things for just three days?" said Allie.

"I'd rather take something and not use it than leave it behind and need it," said Mother. She was folding a shirtwaist, frowning.

"Can I help you?" Allie offered. She looked at her mother wondering what she was thinking, and then realized she was trying to see into her mother's mind, just as Mrs. Pelucci had tried to see into hers. But she could not help it. She felt that things were happening with her mother that might get out of control—that once she was in Manchester, she might make some decision that would be hurtful. Allie wanted to be close to Mother to prevent this if she could, yet she knew that was impossible.

"Why are you staring so?" said Mother now. "You can go and polish my good shoes, if you're so anxious to help. I'll take them in the satchel and wear the other ones on the train."

Allie went and got the shoe polish and the shoes, and tried not to watch her mother so closely—or at least not to let her know she was doing it.

Early the next morning Mother was off to Manchester with her lists and her recipes packed in the satchel along with her clothes. She was in a fine state of nerves when she left, and once she was gone the flat seemed quiet and empty.

Allie and Gertrude fidgeted through the next days. They went to school. They went to Rosa's house. If Allie did not go upstairs to see Mrs. Pelucci of her own accord, Mrs. Pelucci called down to her to come. To her surprise,

191

by the third day Allie was enjoying her conversations with Mrs. Pelucci. Like Rosa, Mrs. Pelucci listened well, and she asked questions that Allie did not object to answering. She asked how Allie fared with the children at the Cobbett Avenue School. She asked about the farm in Nova Scotia, and Allie told of the apple trees beside the lane and the horses in the barn. Allie stopped short of telling about how the horses had been sold, and she did not speak about Papa, but she did finally talk about Aunt Susan and her work, and she did finally tell how she and Gertrude slept in the sewing room. Allie never stayed long with Mrs. Pelucci, but she did not hurry away either.

On Thursday Mrs. Pelucci said, "I think your aunt will miss you if you go to Manchester with your mother. My sister-in-law says she knows your aunt slightly and that she is a lovely lady. She says she has not met your mother."

Again there was the searching that made Allie tense. "Mother has been busy," said Allie. "She has been looking for a position."

"Of course. That is why she is in Manchester. Does she go away often?"

"No. No, this is the first time she has left Boston since ... since we came in December." Allie stood up, feeling wary again and eager to escape. "Mother may be home by now," she said. "Gertrude and I should go and see. She was only going to be in Manchester three days."

She went down to the kitchen, where Gertrude was playing jacks with the younger Raffatini boy. Rosa was watching them, and Mrs. Raffatini was hurrying from the stove to the sink to the cupboard, busy with her endless cooking.

"Allie, you did not have cocoa today," she said. "Sit and I will fix some for you now."

But Allie made her excuses, and when she went home, Mother was not there. She came on Friday, and she glowed with victory. The position was hers. She was to go to Manchester in a week.

"It's a great house," said Mother. "Thank goodness there will be the extra help. Guests come often, and I'm told that many of them are writers and artists. One is the painter who did the portrait of Mr. Reed's late wife. It hangs in the dining room and it's very beautiful.

"And I'm to have an apartment of my own, a bedroom and a little parlor on the top floor. There's a fireplace, so I can have a fire on chilly evenings."

"And what about us?" demanded Gertrude. "Where do we sleep?"

Allie watched her mother's face and saw that Mother was confident and smiling. There was no shadow to dim the great plans. She began to feel safe. Mother had thought of them, or she would not be so calm. Allie felt a stiffness go out of her shoulders. She smiled and sat down at the table, still watching Mother.

"You won't actually be with me at the Reed house," said Mother. "There isn't really a place for you, and I'll be busy, and . . ."

"We won't be taking your time!" cried Gertrude. "We don't need to be looked after as if we were babies!"

"Wait!" said Mother. "Let me finish. There's an academy

not far away that's run by the Sisters of Mercy. You'll be there, you and Allie both. For Allie it will be just as if she'd been entered at the academy in Halifax, and there are classes for younger girls like you, Gertrude. I talked to the Mother Superior. Mr. Reed had his coachman drive me there. Mother agreed that you could enter, even though it will be awkward to have you start in the middle of the year. But Mr. Reed's sister attended the academy, and I think she may have used her influence."

"Oh," said Gertrude.

"There now!" said Mother. She smiled proudly.

Gertrude grinned at Allie. Allie grinned back. They need never see the inside of Cobbett Avenue School again. Rosa would miss them, and Allie would miss Rosa, she knew. But they could write, and perhaps they could visit.

Then Allie saw the look on Aunt Susan's face. It reminded her of the way Uncle Matt had looked the time he bought a gold chain for Aunt Nonie, and Aunt Nonie had scolded him in front of everyone for being extravagant.

"We'll come to see you every summer!" cried Allie.

It was late that night when Allie and Gertrude went to bed, and even then Gertrude was not sleepy. She lay and hugged the blankets as if she feared they would get away from her. "Do you suppose we'll sleep in a dormitory at that academy? With a long row of beds? Like the girls in the story of Elsie Patches at boarding school?"

"I don't know," said Allie. "I wouldn't be surprised."

"It'll be all right so long as it's not the Cobbett Avenue School. Allie, is it true that nuns make you take baths with all your clothes on?"

194

"I don't know. Maybe it is."

"That's dumb."

"Yes."

Gertrude said no more. Allie lay beside her and listened to the rise and fall of voices in the parlor. Mother and Aunt Susan were talking, and doubtless the talk was of Manchester. Doubtless it was Mother who had most to say.

Allie almost wished her mother wouldn't say so much. Aunt Susan had tried so hard to make them happy in Boston, in spite of the fact that the flat was small. Once Susan had suggested that they all stay in Boston and get a bigger flat. Mother had refused. She had been almost rude.

"I'd have to go out and work by the day, and we'd be pinching and scraping along the way I had to when you all went off and left me to look after Mama," she had said. "No thank you. You don't remember what it was like. You couldn't. You were here, doing as you pleased. It was dreadful, and I've had enough. I'll never do it again."

That was it. Mother feared that without Papa, things would be lonely and dull and pinched, the way they had been in that narrow house in Antigonish. The big house in Manchester would not be the same as having Papa, of course. It couldn't be. But it would not be dull and pinched. There would be the appreciation that Mother loved. There would be the maid and the boy who scrubbed, and possibly even Mr. Reed would defer to her. Mr. Reed must think highly of her. He had sent her to see the Mother Superior in his own coach. And so Mother would feel safe and warm. And no matter what Aunt Susan suggested, or how they might manage another way, Mother would go to Manchester. It was decided, and there was no use talking of it.

Nineteen

When Allie woke it was daylight. Gertrude was up and dressed and the room was bright with sunshine.

"Mrs. Pelucci is here," said Gertrude. "She's come to talk with Mother. They want you."

"Mrs. Pelucci?" Allie sat up. "She's here? Is she all right? Yesterday she didn't even come downstairs. What's she doing here?"

"I don't know," said Gertrude.

Then Mother came to see that Allie got out of bed, and she hurried Allie to the parlor. Allie sat in the rocking chair still in her nightgown. Aunt Susan brought her a cup of tea to help her wake up.

"I am sorry, Allie," said Mrs. Pelucci. "Perhaps I come too early. I want to be sure that I talk with you and your mother before too many plans go forward."

Mrs. Pelucci then turned to Mother. "Perhaps it is not

right that sisters be apart from one another. I have seen that Allie and Gertrude are careful one of the other. That is good, eh? Or maybe not always so good. When we grow up at last, we must each be enough for ourselves. If they are so close, perhaps that can make some problems."

Allie looked at Mother. What was happening here? Why was Mrs. Pelucci talking as if Allie and Gertrude might be separated? Mother did not look at Allie. She was watching Mrs. Pelucci. She looked as if she might be curious, but nothing more.

"Allie, I have sent a telegram to my husband." Mrs. Pelucci leaned forward and fixed her dark eyes on Allie's face. "He has agreed to what I ask, but for one, not for two. He is afraid I try for too much. What I try . . . what I want to try . . . is to raise you as if you are my daughter. If you wish, Allie, and if your mother agrees, you can come with me when I go home next week. Or if that is too quick, you can come after."

Allie felt shock. Her hands shook and she quickly put the teacup on the table.

"It is a big decision," said Mrs. Pelucci. "I do not ask you to say this minute whether it will be or not. I can wait for your answer, Mrs. Hughes. So that you are not troubled about the money, I can leave it with you now. You can send Allie after me."

She took an envelope from her purse and put it on the table. "There is enough for the railroad ticket and a little over. And my address."

"Mrs. Pelucci!" Allie stood up. "Listen, I can't . . ."

"Ssshh!" Mrs. Pelucci made a little motion with her

hand. "Do not say anything now. Take time. I hope I do not make an offence. I do not make an offer except for fondness, and loneliness perhaps. We all grow old, and I have just been ill. I know now how it will be to be truly old, and you come to sit beside me, Allie, and that is kind. Do not be afraid. I will make for you a wonderful life—and not the way it was for a girl in the old country. You will have the education. Maybe even college!"

She looked to Mother, and Mother said, "I'll see."

Allie wanted to scream. Why didn't Mother say no straight off? This was mad!

Mrs. Pelucci went out, and Allie watched Mother follow her as far as the top of the stairs. "I'll have to talk about it with Allie," said Mother, "and my sister."

Allie felt she would smother with fury.

Gertrude popped in from the hall just as Mother came back to the parlor.

"A week," said Mother. "I must be in Manchester in a week. It's so little time, and it's such a decision."

"How much time do you need?" Aunt Susan asked. "It doesn't take long to say no."

"But do I want to say no?" said Mother.

"Oh, Mother, yes you do!" cried Allie. "Mother, you can't even think of it. Mrs. Pelucci's . . . she's really a stranger! We really don't know her, and . . ."

"Allie, don't be so hasty," said Mother. "Mrs. Pelucci appears to be a lovely lady, and it might be a wonderful opportunity for you. The education! She talked about college. You could be a teacher!"

"Mother, I don't want college! Mother, don't look away like that. Look at me! Don't you even *care* what I want?"

"You aren't old enough to know what you want," said Mother.

"If Allie's going to St. Louis, so am I!" cried Gertrude.

"Gertrude, you'll go where I send you," said Mother. "Allie, don't carry on so. I thought you liked Mrs. Pelucci. You've spent enough time with her these past days."

"I do like her. I mean, she's all right for an afternoon, but that doesn't mean I want to go and live with her. Besides . . ."

Allie paused, remembering Uncle Hugh's parlor, and stout, talkative Mrs. Cameron being grieved because Aunt Jane was not grateful enough to suit her. Mrs. Pelucci might be a more pleasant lady than Mrs. Cameron, but Allie felt that she would demand her share of gratitude too. And for Allie there might not be anyone like Uncle Hugh who would come and carry her away. Perhaps she would have to stay in St. Louis and be grateful forever.

"I won't go," said Allie.

It was a mistake. It was always a mistake to oppose Mother head-on.

"You are not the one to say what you will do and what you won't," said Mother. "You're only a little girl."

"I'm almost thirteen!"

"You're still a child and you're still obliged to obey. You'll do as you're told!"

"But Mother . . ."

"That's *enough*, Allie. We'll talk about it later."

Allie spun around and went back to the sewing room. Gertrude came after her and shut the door.

"I hate her," said Gertrude.

"You aren't supposed to hate her," said Allie wearily. "She's our mother."

"Then why doesn't she act like a mother?"

Allie began to get dressed, but then she suddenly sat down on the floor in her chemise and her drawers and leaned her head against the bureau. She felt terribly tired.

"Don't go!" said Gertrude. She bent toward Allie and her eyes were fierce. "You don't have to. You can do what Aunt Jane did. Run away!"

"Aunt Jane had Uncle Hugh. She ran away to get married. I don't have anybody to marry."

"All right. If you're going to let her ship you around like some kind of a dumb sheep, I'm not!" Gertrude declared. "And I'm not going to that academy by myself and sleep in a little bed in a long row and take a bath with my clothes on. I'm going to run away."

"Don't play baby games!" said Allie. "You can't run away. Where would you run to?"

Gertrude wasn't discouraged. She wasn't even listening. "Why don't we take the money and hide it," she said. "You know, the money Mrs. Pelucci left for the railroad ticket. And then . . ."

"Then if Mother wants me to go to St. Louis, she'll take the money for the ticket out of the bank. Even if it costs her something in the beginning, she'll save money in the long run. And she'll probably say that I'll thank her for it when I'm older."

Allie did not believe she would ever thank her mother. The future stretched ahead of her like a dark, empty tunnel. What was St. Louis like? What was Mr. Pelucci like? And what would become of Gertrude alone in that school? How could Mother even *dream* of doing this?

Allie got up wearily and finished her dressing. Gertrude was bright, but she hadn't enough common sense. If Allie needed to be saved, she would have to see to it herself.

And with that thought, a plan occurred to Allie. It was a risky plan, but it might work. If she could carry it off she would never go to St. Louis.

She wanted to reach out to Gertrude, to say, "Listen, I've thought of a way," but she didn't. She would say nothing, she decided. Not until she was sure.

As the day went on, Allie was sure.

Her mother would not look at her, and that was not a good sign. She talked around her the way Aunt Nonie used to, and she did not appear to notice whether Allie listened or not.

"Allie might be so much better off," she said. "Of course, I'll have to make inquiries. The Raffatinis seem respectable, but what about Mr. Pelucci? Do you know someone at the bank who might find out more about Mr. Pelucci?"

The remark was addressed to Aunt Susan, who only looked at Mother in a mocking way, as if to say, "Oh, come now, Nell!"

And after a bit Mother said, "Perhaps I could call on Mrs. Raffatini. Yes, I think I had better do that. We can

202

talk about . . . about the family. Didn't Allie say once that Mr. Pelucci owned a factory?"

"Nell, is this really necessary?" said Susan. "Is any of it necessary? I can understand that you might not want to stay in Boston, but couldn't the girls stay here when you go to Manchester? I could put them in the bedroom. It's larger. And I could take the sewing room. I could get a bed that folded up in the daytime."

"How nice!" said Mother. There was an edge to her voice. "You could have two children without the trouble of bearing them. And you'd be the hero of the day. You always liked that."

"What . . . what do you mean?"

"Mama always made such a fuss about you when you came home to Antigonish," Mother went on. "She couldn't be grateful enough that you took the time. The minute you arrived, there was no thought at all of the one who stayed home and did everything. You were the wonderful one, and now you want to play the same game with my children."

Allie felt sick. She wanted to get up and go out of the room, but she was afraid to move—afraid to call attention to herself while Mother was showing these old hurts.

"Nell, I'm sorry." Aunt Susan was white. "I had no idea you felt that way. And . . . and I am not playing a game with your children."

"Yes, you are! You've been doing it since we got here!"

At that Allie heard again that conversation between Mother and Grandma, with Mother crying out that Jane might have a son, and that life wasn't fair.

Mother went into the kitchen now, leaving Allie and Susan to sit in shocked silence. Allie heard pots clatter in the kitchen, and she heard water run in the sink.

She stood up and went to the sewing room. Gertrude was there sulking, sitting on the bed and staring out the window.

Allie shut the door so that Aunt Susan would not hear. She said to Gertrude, "Listen and don't talk. I know what we can do."

Twenty

Aunt Susan's clothes hung in an armoire in the bedroom. There were shirtwaists with high collars and ruffled fronts, skirts trimmed with braid, and jackets with big sleeves. On top of the armoire there were hatboxes.

"Try the blue skirt," said Gertrude. "Aunt Susan doesn't wear it much. Maybe she won't miss it."

"She'll miss it," said Allie, "but by the time she does, it won't matter."

She took down the blue skirt and tried it. It was long, but when she turned the waistband over once it seemed right. The white lawn shirtwaist that Susan wore with the skirt was narrow in the shoulders, but the front was limp and empty, since Susan had a bosom and Allie did not.

"Wait," said Gertrude. She went to the hall where the linens were stored in a bureau. In a moment she came back with a small towel, which she rolled up so that Allie could tuck it inside the shirtwaist. When it was pinned to Allie's chemise, and the shirtwaist was buttoned over it, Allie looked reasonably mature and developed.

"Just don't jiggle too much," warned Gertrude. "You don't want it to come loose."

Allie put on a blue jacket and tried a plaid cape over that. A wide-brimmed black hat finished it off.

But Allie's hair wasn't right. Grown ladies did not wear their hair long and loose and streaming down their backs. Also the hat would not stay on without some some sort of structure to hold it.

Allie put the hat on the bed and set to work with some of Susan's hairpins. It was slippery going. The hair kept sliding away from her and wisping out of the hairpins. Finally she braided it and then pinned the braids up. It was lumpy, but she could anchor the hat with a hatpin.

"Beautiful!" cried Gertrude.

"When we buy the train tickets they'll think I'm a young lady, and you're my niece. If they think about us at all. And why should they?"

Gertrude glowed with delight and plumped herself down on Aunt Susan's bed. "The farm is partly Papa's and partly Uncle Hugh's and partly Uncle Matt's," she said, "so it's partly ours, isn't it? We can live in our old house and cook what we like to eat, and . . . and Allie, do you suppose we can have our own dog?"

"You're being dumb again," said Allie. "They'll never let us live by ourselves. Maybe we can live with Grandma. We could watch out for her, and maybe we could have some of the money from the sawmill so we won't have to be beholden to anybody."

"Grandma would never make us be beholden," said Gertrude.

That was true, and Allie was glad of it, but she knew in her heart that living with Grandma was too simple a solution. No matter what happened, Mother would have the last word. Just the same, Grandma would speak her mind as Grandma always did, and Grandma could make Mother hear.

Allie took off the borrowed things. She put everything back as she had found it. Susan had gone to fit a dress on one of her ladies, and Mother was shopping, so Allie and Gertrude could do as they pleased.

They went to the parlor now, and Allie rummaged in the desk for the timetable Mother had carried with her when they came from Nova Scotia. She found it under some letters and spread it out on the table.

It was confusing. There were columns of figures which turned out to be hours of the day. There were headings for different towns. There were strange little marks and symbols and strange little notes on the back of the timetable and at the bottom. Allie puzzled for some time and finally announced, "There's a train tomorrow. It leaves at ten. Good. It's Sunday and we can leave while Mother and Aunt Susan are at church."

"Why won't we be with them at church?"

"Because we'll be sick in bed. Tonight I'll say I have a headache. Tomorrow I'll act sick and feverish. And I'll say a lot of the kids in school are absent, and one of them broke out with spots before the teacher sent him home. Mother will think they've got something catching, and she'll think I have it too. And you, Gertrude. You've got to be sick."

Gertrude was awed. Allie had suddenly become an accomplished liar. How had she managed it? And would they go to hell for the lies? And for stealing Mrs. Pelucci's money? And missing Mass?

"We're being wicked," said Gertrude. It came out in a frightened whisper.

"We'll make up for it," promised Allie. "Later. When this is over."

Gertrude let herself be comforted. She might be dangling over hell on a slender thread, but hell was a distant place which she had never seen. She had seen Mrs. Pelucci, and Allie would surely go to her if she and Gertrude did not do something to prevent it.

Allie folded the timetable and put it back in the desk drawer. The envelope which Mrs. Pelucci had given Mother was in the drawer, and Allie lifted the flap and saw the money inside. She left it where it was and closed the drawer. "It will be all right," she said, and then did not know whether she said it to assure Gertrude or to comfort herself.

Supper that night was a stiff and silent meal. Mother avoided Susan's eyes. Allie and Gertrude watched their plates and did not look at one another. After the meal they cleared away the dishes. Then they shut themselves in the sewing room, with Allie complaining that her head ached, and Gertrude saying she was tired.

Mother went to bed early. It was only a little past nine when Allie heard her go down the hall. Susan sat late at her sewing. She often did that, and Allie dropped off before Aunt Susan went to join Mother.

Allie woke several times in the night and was awake when Susan got up early in the morning.

"Aunt Susan?" Allie called.

Susan came to the sewing room door and looked in.

"I'm thirsty," said Allie. "I don't feel well." She managed to sound quite weak and woebegone.

Aunt Susan felt Allie's forehead and looked at Allie's throat. "You don't feel feverish," she said.

"My head hurts," said Allie. "Do I have spots?"

"Spots? No. Why?"

Allie told the story of the child at school who had been sent home because he broke out with spots.

"Um," said Aunt Susan. She went and woke Mother.

"Oh, dear," said Mother. "If it isn't one thing it's another."

Mother was not impressed with Allie's symptoms. Just the same, she was mindful of the fact that she had to be in Manchester in a week, and before that time she would have to see Allie and Gertrude settled somewhere.

"Stay in bed now," she said. "Keep warm. Perhaps it will turn out to be nothing."

Gertrude complained that her head hurt too, and she was told to stay quietly with Allie. Aunt Susan brought them a nice breakfast on a tray. There was toast swimming in warm milk, and an egg apiece on top of that. Allie felt horribly guilty, but she ate the egg anyway. Gertrude devoured hers, and the two were very quiet while Mother and Susan got ready for church.

The instant Susan and Mother went out with their rosaries and their prayer books, Allie and Gertrude were up. Gertrude was dressed in no time, but Allie took a little longer. She had to braid her hair and pin on her bosom. While she got herself ready, Gertrude crammed some clothing into their satchels.

They were out and hurrying up the street long before Mother and Aunt Susan could return from Mass. Allie had left a note for her mother. It said, "I can't go to St. Louis," and that was all it could say. Anything more might give them away, and Allie wanted to be safely out of Boston before her mother thought of the train station.

There was a city map in Aunt Susan's desk, and Allie had memorized the way to the train station. They were not halfway there when a streetcar overtook them. They got aboard and the conductor laughed to see them. "Where you going with your mother's hat?" he said. This threw Allie into such confusion that she could hardly pick out the coins to pay their fare. She managed at last, cheeks burning, and he said, "Well now, if the hat looks half as pretty on your mother as it does on you, it looks well indeed."

He went away down the aisle and Gertrude said, "You didn't fool him—but he was nice about it."

"He doesn't have enough to do," snapped Allie.

That was true. The streetcar was almost empty at that hour of a Sunday morning. Allie looked out at the deserted streets and hoped that there would be more people and more hurry at the station. In a crowd no one would notice her or wonder how old she might be.

Even if they did notice her, thought Allie, they probably would not question her. So far as Allie knew, it was not against the law for two young girls to travel. No one could guess that they were using stolen money.

The thought of the money distressed Allie anew. If only they had not had to take the money. Even Grandma, who loved them dearly, even she would not condone the theft of the money. But surely she would help them. She would pay it back for them.

Having thought of Grandma, Allie thought of Mrs. Pelucci. Talking with Mrs. Pelucci had seemed so harmless. When had the idea of taking Allie come to Mrs. Pelucci? Had she made the trip to Boston planning to ask for Rosa? Had the Raffatinis refused her, and had she then turned to Allie? How easy it must have looked to her. There was Allie with no father and with a mother who was hard pressed to make a home for her.

The railroad station appeared at last, and Allie decided to put Mrs. Pelucci out of her mind. She had made her choice, and now there were more important things to think of. She and Gertrude got off the streetcar with their bags and went into the station. There were lots of people. Allie felt safer.

The man at the ticket window hardly looked up when Allie asked for two tickets to Montreal. He took Allie's money and gave her the tickets, and that was the end of it. Allie wondered why she had been so afraid.

"Aren't we going farther than Montreal?" said Gertrude,

after they left the ticket window. "Aren't we going all the way to Nova Scotia?"

"We have to change trains in Montreal, remember? I'll buy the other tickets there. If the police should come here to ask if anybody bought tickets to Antigonish, nobody will remember us."

"Oh," said Gertrude, impressed with Allie's clever criminality.

They found the train without having to ask anyone. There was a notice right next to the big iron gate, and it said the train on Track 14 went to Montreal. It went to a number of other places too, but the end of the line was Montreal.

"We'd better ask the man on the platform to make sure," said Gertrude.

"We'd better not," Allie retorted. She marched down a ramp to the train and got aboard, and Gertrude had to scamper after her or be left.

Allie found seats in a coach. Gertrude sat beside her, stiff and scared, and looked around at the other passengers. They were busy arranging themselves and their luggage and did not seem to notice Gertrude and Allie.

"You sure this is Track 14?" whispered Gertrude. "I could ask that lady there and . . ."

"It's Track 14," said Allie. "It's the right train. Now stop fussing. They'll think there's something wrong."

Gertrude was quiet then, and presently the train chuffed and huffed and gave a great jolt and began to roll.

The conductor started down the aisle shouting for all

passengers to have their tickets ready. Allie's were ready; she had held them in her hand since she bought them.

"Montreal?" said Allie timidly, when the conductor took the tickets.

He must not have heard, for he punched the tickets without answering and went on shouting his way toward the front of the car.

"He didn't hear you," said Gertrude.

"It's all right," Allie insisted. "He punched the tickets."

She turned away from Gertrude and watched out the window at the sooty snow and the large buildings of Boston. It looked as it had when they came, as if the city existed in a perpetual state of grayness and slush. But then there were fewer houses and fewer buildings, and Allie saw fields where the snow was trying to melt itself away in the sunshine.

Soon Boston was gone entirely. Gertrude was asleep, leaning on Allie's shoulder, and Allie was wishing that she could sleep too. She could not. She had to sit erect so long as she wore Aunt Susan's hat, and if she took the hat off she might not be able to get it back on.

She looked past Gertrude, and her eyes met those of the man who sat across the aisle. He was a man with a small chest and narrow shoulders, but he had a big stomach and a face that gleamed red in the cold light that came through the windows. With his head turned toward her, his neck bulged over a stiff collar that was too tight for him.

"Still worried, little missy?" said the man.

Allie did not answer, and he got up and moved to the empty seat behind her. "You're on the right train," he said. "Montreal. I'm not going quite that far, but there's some who'd say that anyplace I go isn't far enough."

He laughed a braying, drunkard's laugh, and his breath gusted against Allie's cheek. She turned her head, trying not to breathe the whisky smell and that other smell that was part stale cigar and part something nasty which the man had eaten.

Gertrude roused herself and looked back. Then she looked ahead again and sat up straight.

"My name's Moore," said the man. "Terrence Moore. My friends just call me Terry."

He laughed again as if he had made a great joke. Then he took a stump of cigar out of his pocket and put it between his teeth.

The conductor had appeared at the end of the car. He took an empty seat and began to shuffle bits of paper.

"Gettin' on for lunch," said Terrence Moore. "Say, li'l lady, maybe you and your . . . your li'l sister would like to join me in the dining car? Have a bite? A li'l nip maybe? But I don't suppose you drink, eh? No, don't suppose so. Say, how old are you, anyway?"

That was a question Allie did not plan to answer. She straightened her spine and looked out the window.

There was the sound of a cork squeaking out of the neck of a bottle, and of liquid gurgling. The man named Terrence Moore swallowed a noisy swallow, and the cork squeaked again. The odor of fresh whisky overlaid the smell of the stale, and of the cigar and whatever else it was that the man had consumed that day.

Then the man was up and standing beside their seat,

and suddenly the whisky he had just taken was a swallow too much. He was unsteady as he reached across Gertrude and tried to take Allie's arm.

"C'mon," he coaxed. "Just a li'l bite in the dining car. I won't . . . won't . . ."

The train swayed. He lurched toward Allie, growing horribly large to her eyes. Gertrude screamed and scrambled from under his arm and out into the aisle.

The conductor was there so quickly that Allie did not see him come. He took the man's arm and led him away. The man went, suddenly meek. And Gertrude was back in her seat and crying with her hands up over her face.

Allie put a hand on Gertrude's arm and watched through a fever of embarrassment and fright as the conductor settled the drunk in a seat at the front of the car. The conductor stayed beside the man for a moment, talking sternly. Then he left the fellow and came back to Gertrude and Allie.

"Sorry, miss," said the conductor. "If that man tries to bother you again I'll put him off at the next stop."

"Thank you," said Allie. She wanted to say it was all right, but it wasn't. She was shaking now with fright and weariness, and a nerve twitched in her cheek.

"Well now," said the conductor, "on second thought, why should he bother you again? Young ladies shouldn't have to contend with the likes of him. Now don't you be unhappy. There's a drawing room empty in the Pullman car, and I'll just move you and your . . . your friend in there and shut the door, and you can have the rest of your journey in peace."

215

Allie was almost more terrified at the thought of a drawing room than at the thought of a drunken stranger. The cost would be staggering!

"We haven't the extra money!" she gasped.

"Don't worry your head," said the conductor. "I'll say a word to the porter, and you be tidy in the place and leave things as you found them, and what harm will there be? And you'll pay nothing extra."

The man's speech was soft, with a lilt to it that reminded Allie of Mr. MacManus. His eyes were clear and the corner of his mouth turned up. Allie smiled at him and then got up, and she and Gertrude followed him down the aisle and through a swaying corridor between cars to the Pullman. The private drawing room was at the far end of the Pullman, and when Allie went in she immediately felt unworthy. There was carpet on the floor that just matched the green plush of the seats. There were light bulbs with little glass shades. There was a clean smell, as if the place had been scrubbed with strong soap, and there were no smudges on the windows.

"Oh!" said Gertrude. "How nice!"

"Thank you," said Allie to the conductor. He smiled at them and then shut the door, and they were safe and secure inside.

They sat facing each other and looking out at the countryside. Now there were stands of dark pine, and sometimes they saw oaks beyond the pine.

"It looks like home," said Gertrude. She sounded happy, as if they must be almost there.

"It's still a long way," said Allie.

"But we're going, Allie. We're really going. Won't Grandma be surprised!"

Allie pictured it in her mind. Grandma would be in the kitchen, and they would come knocking on the door, and she would wonder who it was. And when she opened the door there would be glad cries and hugs, and Rags would bark and jump up on them. And they would all talk at the same time.

And then what would Grandma say?

Allie could not imagine that part. And she could not think how they would explain it all to Grandma.

"Do you think she'll let us stay?" said Gertrude. "Do you really?"

Allie had a feeling of waking from a dream or from a terrible fever. How could she have done it all? She had run away and lied and stolen money. Grandma would have to know of it, and sooner or later she would have to face Mother. She was thankful that Papa would never know. That at least she would be spared. Papa would have been so disappointed.

Allie decided she could think no more about it now. She would put it aside, for she had done all she could. Whatever would be would be.

With that thought came hunger. The breakfast Aunt Susan had fixed for them was only a memory. Allie began to count the money in her purse, and to do fearful calculations about the cost of a meal in the dining car. Then she considered what train tickets from Montreal to Antigonish would cost. And after that there would have to be a carriage to take them from Antigonish to Guysborough. It was horrifying. She decided that they could hardly eat at all on their journey.

"We don't want to have to walk from Antigonish to Guysborough," she told Gertrude. "We might freeze on the way."

Allie had barely uttered this dire prediction when there was a rap at the door. The conductor put his head in to say that the chef in the dining car had fixed too many sandwiches. "You'd oblige him if you'd eat some of them," said the conductor. "The president of the railroad wouldn't approve if we rolled into Montreal with food uneaten."

Allie forgave him instantly for speaking to them as if they were tiny children. She took the sandwiches, which were nicely wrapped in a napkin, and the conductor closed the door and went away.

Allie began to undo the napkin. "We can save some and eat them later," she told Gertrude.

Gertrude sniffed happily. The sight and the smell of food made her brave again. "We're going to be all right, Allie," she said. "You just wait and see."

Twenty-one

The train clacked past processions of switches. "Montreal!" shouted the conductor. "Station is Montreal!"

He opened the door to look in on Allie and Gertrude. "We'll be in the station in a minute," he said. "You young ladies stay here out of sight until the other passengers get off. I'm told there's an inspector for the railroad on the train. I'll get into trouble if he sees you here. I'll come for you when it's safe to leave."

"Oh, dear," said Allie. "I'm sorry if we've . . ."

"No, no!" The conductor held up his hand to stop the apologies. "Don't worry. I'll take care of it."

He disappeared and the door slammed shut. They were rolling slowly now, and Allie and Gertrude could look out at a platform. There were lights, and there was a little knot of men in dark uniforms. Allie took them to be porters. They did not look important enough to be guards.

"Maybe we should pull down the blind so no one can see us," suggested Gertrude.

"No. It might look odd. The conductor said the railroad inspector is on the train anyway, not in the station."

The train jounced to a stop, and Gertrude went to the door and opened it. She put her head out to see the corridor fill with people who had satchels and parcels.

"Gertrude, don't do that!" cried Allie.

Gertrude drew back and almost closed the door. She left a gap of an inch or two and stayed to watch the passengers file past. In a very few minutes the corridor outside the drawing room was empty. The train was very quiet.

And into that quiet came a voice with a soft Irish lilt to it. "Get the guard to come from the station."

It was the conductor talking to someone at the end of the car. The person with the conductor murmured something that Allie and Gertrude could not hear. Then the conductor spoke again. "I can keep them here until you get back," he said. "If they are runaways, the police in Boston may have a report on them. A pair of girls. One looks to be about thirteen, and the other is ten."

Gertrude stepped back and let the door close. "Allie!" she said.

"I heard!"

There was no time to say more. The door opened again and the conductor smiled in on them. "You won't mind staying where you are a bit longer?" he said. "There's a party in the drawing room next door, and they're slow

220

getting their things together. They'll be leaving any minute now."

Allie nodded dumbly and the conductor went away.

"He's sent for a guard," said Gertrude. "They'll send a message, won't they?"

"Probably they'll telegraph," said Allie. She was not terribly surprised. The conductor had been a shade too cheery.

"Do you suppose Mother told the police about us?" said Gertrude. "Will they put us in jail?"

Allie winced. Jail would be unpleasant. And what would happen afterward, when Mother came to claim them, would be even more unpleasant.

"Come on." Allie stood up and opened the door a few inches. Her satchel was in her hand. The corridor was empty. "Don't run," she warned Gertrude. "Someone will notice us if we run."

She took the lead. Gertrude came after her, looking back as she came, fearful that the conductor might appear behind her and seize her. But he was not to be seen, and when they reached the train steps even the porters had gone. They went down to the platform and walked briskly to the gate, and then they darted through and lost themselves in the crowded station.

"What will we do now?" Gertrude wanted to know.

Allie looked at the clock on the station wall. It was almost five. Their train would not go for two hours. "I don't know," she said, "but we can't stay here." She led the way through the station and out the double doors and onto the street. It was dusk, and the street lamps were lighted, and all around them there were cabbies shouting to passengers, trying to get fares. It was like Boston, except that the shouts were in a strange language that Allie took to be French. There was no snow, but a cold wind swept nastily along the ground and whipped at Allie's skirts and tried to snatch the borrowed hat from her head.

"Allie, where are we going?" cried Gertrude.

"Shush!" said Allie, and she forged ahead, away from the station and across a street. She could see the spire of a church against the blue-green sky. If they could reach it without getting lost, there might be a measure of safety there.

They went around a corner into a street where there were tall thin houses like the Raffatini house. Allie looked back toward the station and then looked ahead at the church spire, and decided that they could go straight down this street, and so they did.

Gertrude trotted to keep up, and she grumbled as she did so, and fussed and worried. Allie said, "Sshhh!" a time or two, and then did not listen. Allie was not afraid now. Somehow the path had opened for them so far, and Allie had a sense of being protected. The conductor had put them into the safety of the drawing room. He had fed them. If he had later decided to betray them, what did it signify? Gertrude had chanced to open the door, and they had found out in time.

"You can't trust people," said Gertrude now.

"It wasn't the conductor's fault," Allie told her. "He's a grownup and they don't understand."

"I'm never going to grow up," Gertrude decided. "I'm going to stay the way I am forever."

"There's no point in that," Allie declared. "It just means you'll have to do what other people want forever."

They had reached the church. There were welcoming glints of light behind the stained glass window in the front. "We'll go in here," said Allie, giving the order as if she were the captain of a ship. All day she had been giving orders, and Gertrude had been obeying. She obeyed now, following Allie up the stone steps.

There were double doors and they were closed. They were not locked, and they opened to a vestibule where there was a marble font for holy water. Dutifully Allie and Gertrude blessed themselves. Then they went through inner doors to a quiet dimness that smelled faintly of incense and beeswax. There was a brass rack in front of the altar rail where vigil lights burned green, red, and blue, and the sanctuary lamp was lit.

Allie genuflected and slid into a back pew. Gertrude came after her and sat close.

"We'll wait here," whispered Allie. It was forbidden to talk in church, but they had already sinned so often that day that Allie felt a few whispers in a back pew would not even be noticed by the Lord. "We'll go back to the station and buy the tickets just before it's time for the train." She was glad she had learned the timetable almost by heart.

She thought about going back through the streets to the station, and then to the window where tickets were sold, and she frowned. "If they're looking for us, they'll look for somebody in a plaid cloak and a black hat. Grownup clothes."

Gertrude chuckled. "You didn't fool that conductor. He knew how old you are."

"Yes. But if he has everyone looking for a thirteen-year-old girl who's pretending to be a lady, and I just stop pretending, they won't know it's me!"

She took off Aunt Susan's cloak and folded it and put it down on the seat. Then she stood up and began to take off the hat.

"Allie, wait!" Gertrude clutched her arm.

Somewhere in the church a door had opened.

"Quick!" Allie snatched the cloak. There was a confessional at the side of the church. It was a boxy wooden enclosure that jutted out from the church wall. There was a compartment in the center where the priest would sit, and this had a door. On either side there were compartments that had no doors; they were screened from view only by red curtains that hung almost to the floor.

"In there!" said Allie, and she sped to one of the side compartments. She heard Gertrude stumble into the other side compartment. The kneeling bench in the confessional creaked as Gertrude went to her knees, as if there were a priest in the little central place and she had come to have her sins forgiven.

Allie leaned against the back of the confessional and realized that she had given way to a moment of panic. She had been afraid that she and Gertrude would be questioned. Someone would ask why they were in the church. She could have said simply that they had come in to say a prayer. But if they were discovered hiding in a confessional, she would never be able to explain.

Footsteps came along the aisle. Then more light showed through the chink between the curtain and the confessional. She bent toward the chink and saw a priest with a taper fixed on the end of a long pole. He was lighting the oil lamps that hung from the ceiling by long chains. When he finished with this, the darkness was driven back to the corners of the church.

Allie saw him snuff out his taper and start toward the confessional. She drew back and heard his footsteps, and then the door to the priest's compartment opened. The priest stood just outside the door and hummed softly, and she heard him fumbling in the middle compartment. Then he stopped humming and the door shut. The footsteps went away toward the front of the church.

Again Allie looked out between the curtain and the side of the confessional. She saw that the priest was pacing up and down the center aisle with the book open, his lips moving in silent prayer. He was saying his office. He had come to the confessional only to get his breviary.

Allie knelt. That was the most comfortable thing to do in a confessional. They were safe for the moment. She put her head against the grill that separated her compartment from the priest's place, and she heard Gertrude stirring on the far side of the booth. They waited, listening to the footsteps in the church and smelling the odor that seemed always to haunt confessionals. It was a mixture of stale air and dust and something else, which Allie took to be repentance.

Time went by and Allie thought of the train. How long had they been there? She shifted and looked out through the gap in the curtain. There was the priest, still pacing. When she tugged the curtain slightly she could see the railing of the choir loft where there was a clock. Only half an hour had passed. It had seemed longer.

The priest closed his book at last and went toward the front of the church. Allie heard a door open and close. He was gone.

But then another door opened, and a woman's voice sounded shockingly loud in the church. It was a scolding voice, and the language was foreign. Allie peeped out.

An old woman whose head was covered with a shawl came holding a child by the hand. Down the aisle she went, talking on and on, and at the front of the church she stopped next to the brass rack where the vigil lights burned.

The woman had numbers of loud things to say about the lights, or possibly about the child who was with her. When she finished saying these things a coin dropped into a box on the brass rack. The woman lit a candle, then lifted the child up so that he could light one. She knelt, crossing herself with ferocious piety, and Allie heard the mumble of a prayer. The prayer was interrupted every few seconds so that the woman could poke at the child or force his hands together in a reverent attitude. He endured this without a whimper, and when the woman had finished he let her take his hand and hurry him out of the church. His small face was as blank as a new page in a copybook.

Allie and Gertrude crept out of the confessional when

the church was quiet again. They did not speak as Allie took off Aunt Susan's hat and undid her braids. She let her hair fall free, and she put the rolled up towel that had filled out her blouse into her bag. The hat was hidden in the confessional, and Aunt Susan's skirt was turned over twice at the waistband. When it hung in uneven folds just above her ankles she turned the cloak inside out so that only the red lining showed when she put it on.

"How do I look?" she said to Gertrude.

"Better," said Gertrude. "Before you looked as if you were playing dressup."

Allie turned to the altar and said a quick prayer. It would have been rude not to. Then she and Gertrude went out to the dark street and back to the hurry and bustle of the train section.

It was ten minutes before train time when Allie bought the tickets. She and Gertrude went to the gate and stood behind a man who was just showing his ticket to the guard. The guard nodded to the man and he went through the gate and strode off down the platform.

"Wait for us!" cried Allie.

The man looked around, frowned a puzzled frown, then went on.

"On with you," said the guard. "Catch up with your dad."

They went down the platform and found the coach and were sitting on a seat at the end of the car when the conductor cried his "All aboard!"

The train began to move. Allie looked at Gertrude. "Soon," she said. "We'll soon be there."

* * * * * *

It was morning when the train chugged into the station in Antigonish. Allie and Gertrude climbed down onto a platform that was not in the least like the platforms in Boston or in Montreal. It was made of bare wooden planks and it was open to the wind. They were the only passengers to get off, and when they looked around they saw no hurrying crowds and no shouting cabbies, but only the shops and the houses of a country town.

"I'm cold," said Gertrude. "What do we do now?"

Allie was not sure of the next step, so they went into the station house to get out of the cold while she decided. The place smelled of tobacco and hot metal, with the stove in the corner almost glowing. They warmed themselves, turning in front of the stove and holding out their hands.

"We should get something to eat," said Allie. "I wonder if there's a place where we could have a cup of tea."

She thought of the teas they had had with Mother, and the slices of cake heavy with currants. She thought of toast kept warm under a napkin and the saliva came to her mouth. Allie was not just hungry; she felt she was starving.

A man with a green eyeshade looked out from a little window on the far side of the room. "Are you girls waiting for someone?" he said. He looked worried, as if there might not be enough heat in the stove to keep all three of them warm.

"My grandfather is coming for us," said Allie, who could now tell lies almost without thinking.

The man stayed in the window, and it seemed to Allie

that his was a piercing and suspicious gaze, so Allie plucked Gertrude by the sleeve, and the two went out before the man could ask more questions.

There was a shop across the way where sausages hung in the window, and loaves of bread were piled underneath like so many wooden logs. Allie and Gertrude went in and bought some of the bread and some cheese and a sausage. The shopkeeper was as curious as the man at the station. He had seen them get off the train, he said, and wondered where they were going. When Allie repeated the fib about the grandfather who would come to meet them, he offered to let them wait in the shop.

Allie sensed a trap, but there was no way to refuse. Besides, the street was cold.

The stove was not as glowing as the one in the station, but it was comfortable when one edged close to it. The bread was stale, but it was delicious. Allie and Gertrude ate some of the cheese, which was hard. They passed the sausage back and forth and nibbled the ends, since there was no way to cut it. The shopkeeper went into the back of his shop, and Allie heard a door open. A draft gusted through the shop and the door closed again.

"He's going to ask the man at the station about us," said Gertrude.

She was right. They looked out past the sausages and saw the shopkeeper come around from the back of his building and cross the street to the station.

Allie felt tired enough to sit down where she was and die. She reasoned that the man at the station and the shopkeeper would confer. They would decide that the story of the grandfather was unlikely. Antigonish was a place that was bigger than Guysborough, but not that much bigger. If one of the townsfolk had been expecting a pair of granddaughters to get off the train, the man at the station might have expected to know of it.

Or perhaps there had already been a wire from Montreal or even from Boston. Mother would have guessed they would come this way.

"Gertrude, they know!" said Allie. "They've been waiting for us!"

"Is there a jail in Antigonish?" said Gertrude. Her voice quavered.

"We won't go to jail," Allie promised. "We'll hide."

"We can't hide forever."

"We'll hide until it gets dark. Then we'll walk until we find a place to sleep, like a barn. Then when it gets light we'll walk some more. We've come this far. I'm not going to give up now."

They went out through the back, as the shopkeeper had gone. There was a rutted, muddy lane behind the building. At the end of the lane there was a street where small houses stood in a row, and beyond that row was a building that looked like a barn.

"There!" said Allie. "It's going to be all right."

"It'll be cold," said Gertrude. "Couldn't we find a church like the one in Montreal?"

"Somebody would see us," Allie pointed out.

She started for the barn, and for once she did not look back to make sure Gertrude was following. But suddenly there was a dog in front of her. It was a lean, ugly, white creature with pink patches on its hide where the fur had been scratched away. It stood in Allie's path, stiff and watchful, and it growled.

"Nice boy," said Allie.

She moved a step forward and the dog growled again.

Then there was a rattling of wheels behind Allie and Gertrude, and the sound of hoofs. The dog looked away from Allie. It dropped its head and moved to one side.

"Whoa!" cried the driver of the wagon. "Easy theah! Whoa!"

Allie turned about. She looked up at a dark-skinned man whose face was shaded by his hat brim. The light was behind him, and for an instant she could not be sure of the face. But then he spoke again and she knew.

"Mah goodness!" said the soft, deep voice. "Miss Allie, what you doin' here? An' Miss Gertrude! Your mama know you here all by yoselfs? Miss Allie, where is your mama anyway?"

Joe Johnson got down from the wagon, and suddenly Allie was hugging him around the middle and crying as if she would never stop.

Twenty-two

The barn at the end of the street was really a livery stable, and Joe worked there. Now he found a place for Allie and Gertrude in an empty stall. He got clean straw for them so that they could snuggle down and be warm. He took a blanket from his bed, which was in the loft, and he spread the blanket on top of the straw.

Allie and Gertrude ate their bread and cheese and sausage. They sipped tea from a heavy china mug which they passed back and forth between them. Joe had brewed the tea until it was almost black, and then had sugared it until it was almost syrup. It was hot and heartening and delicious.

Joe watched them eat and drink. When they had finished he took the mug and set it aside. "Now what do all this mean?" he said. "Where is your mama?"

"We ran away," said Gertrude. "Mother was going to sell Allie to Mrs. Pelucci."

Joe shook his head. "White people don sell each other! White people don even sell black people no more."

"Well, not sell exactly," said Gertrude. "Mother wanted to give Allie away."

Joe looked unbelieving.

Allie then tried to explain. She told how Mrs. Pelucci had no children, and how she had asked if Allie might come and live with her."

"And I would have had to go away to school all by myself!" Gertrude added. "Maybe I'd never see Allie again. And Mother didn't care!"

Allie knew they were being traitorous to Mother and she had a moment of guilt. But then she felt a bitter resentment; Mother hadn't worried greatly about her feelings.

"Where this lady live who want to take you, Miss Allie?" questioned Joe.

"St. Louis!" snapped Gertrude. "Far away!"

"Far away fo' sure!" said Joe. "I know St. Louis. I been there!"

"That's why we're running home to Grandma," said Gertrude.

Joe was relieved to hear it. "Miz Hughes, she'll know what to do," he said. "Recon I kin take you if you kin wait 'til tonight. The man who owns this stable, he'll len' me a wagon, only you got to hide in the wagon out a sight 'cause no tellin' what some folks think if'n they see a black man on the road with two little girls."

233

So it was settled. Allie and Gertrude stayed the day in the stall, out of sight and very quiet. Allie slept and waked, then slept again. Sometimes she dreamed and some of the dreams were of Papa, and once in her dream she and Gertrude were in Canso, standing on the dock and looking out over the water. They could see the island, and they knew that Grandma was there waiting for them, but they could not get to her for they had no boat.

But then Allie woke and knew that it was a foolish jumble, like most dreams, and Joe would take them to Grandma.

It was almost dark when Joe brought more sausage and bread and more tea, and he told them the man who owned the stable had agreed to lend him a horse and the wagon. "I tell him I'm goin' to do some haulin' for a farmer out in the countryside, and I'll be gone two days. He don like it much, but not much he can do about it. Ain't too many people in these parts got time free to help with the horses."

Lying did not seem to cause Joe any distress. He did it with ease, and as he helped them into the back of the borrowed wagon and covered them with his blanket, he told them of the day just past. The man at the station had indeed had information from Montreal that the Hughes girls from Guysborough might come this way, and they were to be detained.

"That mean they put you someplace an' lock the door!" said Joe.

"Like jail?" asked Gertrude.

"Someplace safe, jes till your mama come. They ask me if'n I seen you, an' I said no. Lucky they don know I

234

knows your mama an' your grandma. Ain't never a good idea to let folks know too much, so I jes never tell 'em."

Joe gathered the reins and clucked to the horse, and they lumbered away from the stable and down the street and out of Antigonish. When they were clear of the place at last, Joe turned to look at Allie.

"You grieved your mama, Miss Allie, you know that?"

Allie knew it, but she did not know what else she could have done. Mother had shut herself into her own grieving for Papa until she could do nothing but grieve and be anxious. Allie could not talk to her. She did not listen, and she did not see that Allie grieved too.

"Grandma will say we did right," said Gertrude.

"An' if she do?" said Joe. "Your grandma be your grandma, but your mama be your own mama. It ain't right to grieve your mama."

They talked no more of it then. Joe was not one to wear a thing out with too many words. It grew really dark, and they went on with the wind blowing fresh on them. Allie knew that freshness. It came from the open sea. She lay looking up at the sky, which was velvet black between the stars. The moon came out and then the night was not so dark. Allie tried to make her mind empty so that she could not remember the year past, so filled with hurt.

They went over the back lanes, past farms and fields, and then through the high country to the east of the Intervale. It was still dark when they rumbled down the road and turned onto the lane that went past the sawmill. Allie sat up in the wagon. She saw that fog had come from the sea to settle thick in the low places, and she remembered how this was always true.

They went up the lane. The house where Allie had been born was a dark square beside the road. She reached to touch Joe's arm and she did not have to speak. Joe stopped the wagon so that she could look as long as she needed to, and in that first faint light before dawn she saw that boards had been nailed over the windows. She tried to remember the kitchen, warm from the fire and filled with the smells of cooking, but the memory would not stay in her mind. Instead she saw again the furniture covered with sheets and the beds stripped and empty. It was what they had come to because Papa was dead.

"All right," said Allie to Joe. "We can go on."

They went up past the barn, and Allie heard the animals stir inside and saw a light gleam from a window. Grandma must have someone living there, perhaps sleeping in the stall that had been fixed for Joe. She was glad. Grandma should not be by herself on the place.

There was light in the big house at the top of the lane. The journey was ending at last. Allie shook Gertrude, and Gertrude sat up and saw the light, and a great longing was suddenly in her face.

Joe reined in the horse at Grandma's gate, and Grandma's door opened. Allie and Gertrude scrambled down and ran to the tiny upright figure in the doorway, whale-bone stiff and swathed in her big morning apron. Grandma had a skillet in her hand, and when she saw who had come she let it drop. It bounced down the steps and rolled away. Grandma clutched Gertrude and then was folded in Allie's arms.

Joe waited in the darkness and tears were shed, and if some of them were Joe's, no one need notice.

"I knew it!" Grandma cried. "You've come back. I knew you would! You wouldn't stay way off there and ..." Grandma stopped. She looked to the black man. "Joe? Is that you?"

"Yes'm, Miz Hughes."

Her eyes went to the girls then. "Where is your mother?"

"I ... I suppose in Boston." Allie almost choked as she said it.

"She was going to give Allie away," said Gertrude, and the words came out in a rush and a tumble. "Allie was going to have to live with Mrs. Pelucci in St. Louis, and I might never see her again—and we don't even know whether the Peluccis speak English when they're home."

That made nothing clear to Grandma. But Grandma did see that the trouble, whatever it was, would not be easily settled. Perhaps she decided no one should hurry the settling of it, for she told Joe to put the horse in the barn, and then come back to the house. She shepherded the girls into the kitchen, and there was real warmth at last. Gertrude went right to the stove and turned her back to get warm, and Allie sat down suddenly in Grandma's own chair and felt the luxury of it. She thought of the strange places they had slept in the past days, and the cold and the hunger—and the fear.

"Something to eat," said Grandma, "and some sleep, and we'll see."

Presently Joe came into the kitchen, and Ted Maginnis came after him. Maginnis was a man who had idled about in Guysborough for as long as Allie could remember, doing a turn now and again at chopping wood or helping paint a house. So it was he who slept in Grandma's barn these days. Allie grinned. He would not be idle if Grandma could prevent it. This morning he was clumsy and stumbled over the doorsill in his astonishment at seeing Allie and Gertrude.

"Dinna you be standin' there like a great gowk!" scolded Grandma. "Go and light a fire in the corner bedroom. Then come for your breakfast, for you must go to Guysborough to get Matt Hughes."

Maginnis did as he was told, and Allie and Gertrude ate and then were led upstairs. Allie went to bed in her petticoat, for it didn't seem worth the trouble to try to find her nightdress. The last thing she saw before she dropped off to sleep was Grandma sitting beside the bed with her rosary in her hand and her old face sad. Allie knew that she might not be praying. She might only be keeping still. It was a way she had when there was trouble. She did not want to fret at it, but to wait and let the answer come of itself.

* * * * * *

In two days Mother was there. Uncle Matt had sent a wire to let her know the girls were with Grandma. She had wired back that she was coming, and Maginnis had gone to Antigonish to meet the train and drive her back to the farm.

238

She was stiff with fury when she got down from the carriage. She swept up the steps and into the parlor and sat with her face white as chalk and her dark eyes snapping.

"How could you?" she said to Allie. "I didn't sleep a wink for two nights. Half the police in Boston were looking for you. You shamed me! And I had to write to Mr. Reed and put him off. And Mrs. Raffatini heard what you'd done and came to inquire, and then she wrote to Mrs. Pelucci. If you think you're welcome in that house any longer after this, you had better think again!"

"Good!" cried Gertrude. She was now in a state of complete defiance. "Allie doesn't want to be in her old house!"

"Hold your tongue!" cried Mother.

Grandma shook her head at Gertrude. "It will not do to speak so," she warned.

But Grandma did not look angry. Indeed, there was a trace of a smile on her face as she turned to Mother. "Since the grand lady who would take Allie needs naught but a tame heifer," she said, "the thing has settled itself. Allie cannot go to her, so she must bide away from her."

Allie's heart lifted. She wanted to hug Grandma.

But Mother would have none of this sort of talk. "It was a marvelous opportunity," she declared. "Allie would have had everything."

"Aye, everything but wha' she should have," said Grandma. "Her own flesh and blood close by her, and her own place where she is by right, and not wi' strangers who would have her fill a place empty in their own lives."

"Is it so wrong to fill a place in someone's life?" Mother demanded. "Isn't that what everyone wants?"

"If it is a choice, 'tis a brave one, but if it is a thing one is forced to, 'tis a different thing entirely."

There was the sound of a carriage in the lane. " 'Tis Hugh who comes," said Grandma, "and Matt. Allie and Gertrude are their brother's children, and 'tis right that they be here this day."

Mother stood up and held her head high. "I will always be glad to see them," she said evenly.

Allie doubted that. She might well have been saying that Uncle Matt and Uncle Hugh could come or stay away, and it was all the same to her, for Allie and Gertrude were her children, not theirs.

But when Uncle Hugh came in, Aunt Jane was with him, and Mother lowered her eyes and looked away. After Uncle Hugh, Uncle Matt came. Aunt Nonie was close behind him, for how could one escape bringing Nonie?

Mother groaned. "Why didn't you ask Mrs. Anderson to come too?" she cried. "Why didn't you have the whole parish in? It doesn't become you, Mother, to make such a spectacle of us."

Grandma gave no sign that she even heard this; she was watching Aunt Jane, who started toward Allie and Gertrude as if she would kiss them, and then hesitated as if she could not be sure it was the right thing to do, and then turned away looking troubled.

Aunt Jane sat down, and Aunt Nonie shot a sour glance at her. And then Nonie announced in her flat-footed way that there was no need for Allie and Gertrude to go to strangers. She and Matt could take them.

"The girls are not orphans, you know," said Mother.

"I know that," said Nonie, "but there's some who seem to have forgotten it."

Nonie sat down, and Allie saw that her smile was filled with malice and satisfaction. There had never been any love lost between Mother and Aunt Nonie. It must give Nonie pleasure now to see Mother brought low.

"Passing out children as if they were stray kittens," Aunt Nonie chided.

Gertrude moved closer to Allie and took her hand.

"How dare you!" cried Mother. "It isn't that way at all!"

"Then how is it, Ellen?" said Grandma. "Tell us."

"I want the best for Allie," said Mother. "I want the best for them both, and for all of us. It was practical and wise and . . ."

"Ellen, if you needed money . . ." Grandma began.

"It wasn't only the money!" cried Mother. "That was part of it, it's true. But I have no place where I can manage, and plan, and no one to cook for. And in Boston no people come and go . . ."

Aunt Jane had been sitting quiet, unmoving, but Allie saw her look around now, out the window and down the lane. She was looking at the house that was closed and empty. It had been Mother's house, and it could be still.

But Mother had seen Jane's look too. "No!" she cried. "I can't stay here!"

Allie's heart wrenched. She knew her mother spoke only

241

what was true. She could not stay in the house that Papa had built for her. Not without Papa. And she could not live as Susan lived, in her own corner with only a neighbor now and then, and the boys who came from the butcher or the grocer. She could not live without someone to pay attention when she spoke. Mother needed appreciation. "You do well for a sea captain's daughter," Papa had always told her, and that was why she had done well for him.

Allie wondered if Mr. Reed had told her how well she did. When she cooked for him and saw to the serving of his meal, what did he say? Something that pleased her, no doubt, and so she would go to manage his house.

The truth of the matter was that Papa was dead, and Mother could not turn from her grief as Grandma did to keep close to the ones who were left. Mother could not love Allie and Gertrude as she had when Papa lived. Now if she saw any bit of him in Allie and Gertrude, it was a pain to her, not a comfort. It angered her, and if that was a kind of wickedness, she might not be able to help it. She might not even know it.

Allie heard Grandma say, "Well, then, what now? What will ye have the girls do?"

Mother looked suddenly bent and pinched, but then she took a breath and sat straighter. "I've spoken to Mr. Reed, and he will wait until I can make arrangements and see the girls settled. Allie and Gertrude will go together to the academy. They won't be far from me. In the summers there is Susan in Boston, and . . ."

"And Hugh and I," said Aunt Jane. Though she was

big with her child, she rose up lightly from her seat. "We'll be glad to have Allie and Gertrude, truly. For all of the summers, or part, whenever they wish. It would be a pleasure to me!"

She came to Allie then and did kiss her. "You would never have to be grateful," she said. "Not for a minute."

Allie knew that she remembered how it had been when first they met. It seemed so long ago now.

And so it was settled. The uncles and aunt stirred themselves. Aunt Nonie sniffed at the girls and told them to be good, and she and Uncle Matt went off in their buggy, which had managed to become tired and creaky in the short time that they had had it. Poor Aunt Nonie. The dreariness rubbed off on everything she touched. And poor Uncle Matt, who was graying and solemn these days, but who bore what he had to bear.

Uncle Hugh had been quiet through it all, but now he came and hugged Allie and then Gertrude. Then he and Aunt Jane went out to see what changes there might be on the farm. When they were gone, and when Mother had taken herself up the stairs to set herself right after her journey, Grandma took Allie's hand.

"I am easier in my mind," said Grandma. "It was a fearful thing ye did, Allie. It could have ended so badly. Thanks be to God it did not. And dinna be hard on your mother. She was e'er a fine wife to your father, and wi' that let us be content."

Allie nodded, and Gertrude, who had been very quiet, came to hug Grandma. Mother came down the stairs, and Grandma went to get her something to eat. For a little while it felt as if they had just run up the lane to visit for the afternoon. Soon Papa would come from Halifax or Canso, and he would be filled with great and wonderful plans.

It was not so. Allie felt it like a pain. But also she knew the pain would pass for her, and so she could bear it.

Twenty-three

The letter came on a sunny afternoon in May. Mother Superior brought it upstairs to Allie, who was sitting on a windowsill looking out. She had a book open on her lap, but she had not even tried to read. There was an apple tree in bloom on the far side of the lawn, and nearer, the crocuses were showing in the grass.

"Are you studying, my dear?" asked Mother Superior.

Allie jumped, looking guilty, and dropped the book. It thumped to the floor and lay there face down.

"Never mind," said Mother Superior. "Who could study on a day like this?"

Mother Superior bent and picked up the book. Allie had never seen her do such a thing before. Mother Superior did not pick things up for anyone. People picked things up for Mother Superior.

Allie stood up respectfully, and the nun sat down on the windowsill in the place Allie had vacated.

"I have some news," said Mother. "Bring that chair, Mary Alice, and sit here beside me."

Allie felt a fright, but she did not question. She brought the chair.

There must have been a letter, she thought. Of course Mother Superior knew what was in it. She opened all the letters. She read the stiff notes that Aunt Nonie sent. They were dull and filled with complaints about the high price of everything. She read the letters that came from Mother. They were oddly impersonal and told of menus and entertainments at Mr. Reed's big house.

Mother Superior also read Grandma's letters, and these were jumbles of loving wishes and accounts of the wicked behavior of Rags the dog. They were also filled with praise for Jane's baby, who had been born late in April. He was so like Hugh, wrote Grandma, that sometimes Grandma felt she might have born him herself.

Aunt Jane wrote seldom. She had no time, with Kathleen married to Mr. MacManus and gone away. Jane was managing her own house now, and the baby besides. She had to teach a new Irish girl to cook when she scarcely knew how herself. Still, she did write occasionally, and the letters were filled with a love that had grown strong between Allie and Jane since Allie's great adventure.

This afternoon it was a letter from Jane that Mother Superior took from one of the many pockets concealed in her flowing black habit. Allie recognized the neat, schoolgirl hand.

246

"Where is Gertrude?" Mother Superior asked. She said it as Mother might once have said it.

"She went out with some of the younger girls," Allie answered. "They said they'd pick wild flowers to put on Our Lady's altar."

"She's pious all of a sudden," said Mother Superior. "Never mind. It won't last, and while she's picking wild flowers she isn't apt to get into too much trouble. A case of poison ivy, perhaps, but that's the worst of it."

Mother suddenly looked concerned. Her heavy, doughy face was sad. "Is Gertrude happy here?" she asked.

"I think so," Allie told her, knowing that at that moment Mother Superior considered her almost the same as Gertrude's parent. "She's as happy as she can be right now. She doesn't like having to keep so neat all the time though."

"I hadn't noticed that she does keep neat," said Mother. "Oh, well, there are more important things."

The sisters encouraged restraint and did not approve of impatience, so Allie had not asked about the letter in Mother's hand. Mother unfolded it now and handed it to Allie.

"I'll stay with you for a few minutes," she said.

At that, Allie knew what the news would be.

She looked down at the sheets of paper.

"Dear Allie," she read, "and Gertrude too, there is no good way to tell you what has happened, so I will tell you quickly and right away. Your grandmother died on Tuesday evening last, very quietly. She felt ill early in the day and sent Ted for your Uncle Matt and Aunt Nonie. Ted came on to Canso then to get Hugh and me. She was still awake when we reached the farm. She knew that she was dying and she told us she had always wanted to go with her bairns all about her. That was the way she said it. She said the priest had told her that in heaven we know our own and soon she would be with your father and grandfather. She told us to see that nothing happens to the Hughes land, and we will do that. She died then, and it was so easy that we did not know it at first. It was only that she stopped talking, and after a bit the doctor touched her wrist and told us it was over and we were very fortunate.

"She was buried on Thursday in the churchyard next to your grandfather. Hugh is having a stone made with her dates. I will miss her very much. We could not see her often, but I think she loved me and I know she loved you.

"I will write again in a day or two. I cannot sit still now for very long. The baby cries or the girl who came to take Kathleen's place drops things. Do not be sad, and come to us when school is over. You will love our baby."

Allie finished reading. She folded the letter, and she was surprised when her eyes blurred and the tears fell. She had not been able to cry for Papa until long after his death. Now she cried so easily for Grandma, and she had loved Grandma dearly, but now the pain was not so great and there was no anger.

"There now," said Mother Superior. She took Allie's hand. "I remember when my grandmother died."

Allie was surprised. The sisters were supposed to leave their old lives behind when they made their vows. She had never heard one of them talk of home and family before.

But of course they could not leave everything. Vows or no vows, there had to be memories.

"I was a raw farm girl," said Mother Superior, "and my grandmother was a cranky old lady who lived in the room at the top of the stairs. She pounded on the floor with her cane when she wanted something, and how we all would jump. And how we cried when she died. She was my mother's mother."

The nun went on to talk softly of her life with her family, and after a minute or two Allie didn't listen. It was enough that she was there with her big calm face and her black garments and the soft voice going on and on. In her way she was saying what Grandma would have said if she were here. The Lord giveth and the Lord taketh away, blessed be the name of the Lord.

The tears passed. Mother Superior let go of her hand. The younger girls were laughing in the corridor below, and there were footsteps on the stairs.

"Well, now," said Mother Superior.

"I'll tell Gertrude," said Allie.

"Yes. Later you and Gertrude can come to my parlor for tea. I'll expect you at five."

"Yes, Mother."

Mother went out, majestic as a great ship. Gertrude passed her in the doorway and bobbed a careless curtsy. Her hair was as tangled as ever, and there was a button gone from the front of her shirtwaist. She was taller now, and her face was thinner. She still raged at times, but not so often as she once had.

She might rage now for a while, but it would pass

quickly. Allie would listen and not attempt to quiet the rage, and it would be over.

"What's the matter?" Gertrude said now. "You look funny."

Allie held the letter out to her. She took it and sat on the windowsill and began to read.

Until 1969, MARY CAREY was on the staff of the Disney Studio in Burbank, California. "When I came to California from New York, I didn't really plan to go to work for Disney," she says, "but I wanted to see what the studio looked like. Applying for a job was a keen way to get past the front gate, so I applied. They hired me, and that proves that life is indeed what happens to you while you're making other plans."

She left the studio after fifteen years and became a full-time freelance writer. She has done many books for children; this is her first for Dodd, Mead.

Today she lives in a small community not far from Los Angeles, where she can be a part-time beachcomber when she isn't writing.